HARLE
Pre

Welcome to the February 2009 collection of Harlequin Presents!

This month read the final installment of Lynne Graham's trilogy VIRGIN BRIDES, ARROGANT HUSBANDS, *The Spanish Billionaire's Pregnant Wife.* Leandro Marquez ruthlessly stops at nothing to wed Molly when he discovers she's pregnant with his child! And don't miss the first part of our fabulous new series INTERNATIONAL BILLIONAIRES, which starts when shy, hardworking Holly is swept off her feet by the magnificent Prince Casper in Sarah Morgan's *The Prince's Waitress Wife.* Expect emotions to reach fever pitch in Carole Mortimer's *The Mediterranean Millionaire's Reluctant Mistress* when tycoon Alejandro is determined to claim his secret baby and possess Brynne in the process. And will an innocent plain Jane convince Sheikh Tair Al Sharif to let go of his mistrustful nature in Kim Lawrence's *Desert Prince, Defiant Virgin?* Business tycoon Santos Cordero is intent on seducing Alexa into a marriage of convenience in Kate Walker's *Cordero's Forced Bride,* while sexual tension heightens when Stefano seeks revenge after being left at the altar in Kate Hewitt's *The Italian's Bought Bride.* Be prepared for a battle of the sexes in Robyn Grady's *Confessions of a Millionaire's Mistress* as Celeste and Ben find they want the same thing in the bedroom…but different things from life! Plus, look out for Nicola Marsh's *The Boss's Bedroom Agenda,* in which a sizzling night spent together between Beth and her gorgeous new boss, Aidan, changes everything!

We'd love to hear what you think about Harlequin Presents. E-mail us at Presents@hmb.co.uk, or join in the discussions at www.iheartpresents.com and www.sensationalromance.blogspot.com, where you'll also find more information about books and authors!

Bedded by...

Blackmail

Forced to bed...then to wed?

He's got her firmly in his sights and she's got
only one chance of survival—surrender to his
blackmail...and him...in his bed!

Bedded by... **Blackmail**

The *big* miniseries from Harlequin Presents®.

Dare you read it?

Kate Walker

CORDERO'S
FORCED BRIDE

Bedded by... 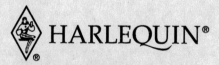 Blackmail
Forced to bed...then to wed?

HARLEQUIN®

TORONTO • NEW YORK • LONDON
AMSTERDAM • PARIS • SYDNEY • HAMBURG
STOCKHOLM • ATHENS • TOKYO • MILAN • MADRID
PRAGUE • WARSAW • BUDAPEST • AUCKLAND

Recycling programs
for this product may
not exist in your area.

ISBN-13: 978-0-373-12799-3
ISBN-10:   0-373-12799-5

CORDERO'S FORCED BRIDE

First North American Publication 2009.

www.eHarlequin.com

Printed in U.S.A.

All about the author...
Kate Walker

KATE WALKER was born in Nottinghamshire, England, and grew up in a home where books were vitally important. Even before she could write she was making up stories. She can't remember a time when she wasn't scribbling away at something.

But everyone told her that she would never make a living as a writer, so she became a librarian instead. It was at the University of Wales, Aberystwyth, that she met her husband, who was also studying at the college. They married and eventually moved to Lincolnshire, where she worked as a children's librarian until her son was born.

After three years of being a full-time housewife and mother, she was ready for a new challenge, so she turned to her old love of writing. The first two novels she sent off to Harlequin were rejected, but the third attempt was successful. She can still remember the moment that a letter of acceptance arrived instead of the rejection slip she had been dreading. But the moment she truly realized that she was a published writer was when copies of her first book, *The Chalk Line*, arrived just in time to be one of her best Christmas presents ever.

Kate is often asked if she's a romantic person, since she writes romances. Her answer is that if being romantic means caring about other people enough to make that extra-special effort for them, then yes, she is.

Kate loves to hear from her fans. You can contact her through her Web site at www.kate-walker.com, or e-mail her at kate@kate-walker.com.

For Helen

CHAPTER ONE

IF SHE WAS going to do this, then she had better get on with it, Alexa told herself firmly. In fact, she had better get on with it *right now*, she added fiercely, knowing there was no other way forward.

Because the truth was that she *did* have to do this. Somebody had to, that was for sure. No one else was going to do it. And definitely not Natalie.

Natalie would never have coped with this. She'd have given in, gone down under pressure, and she'd have ended up saying the exact opposite of what she'd come to say—what she *needed* to say.

If Natalie had had to face Santos Cordero then she would have agreed to go through with this wedding she didn't want, just as she'd been agreeing to do right from the start. She'd go through with it and as a result she'd miss out on her chance of a real relationship, real love. No, Natalie was better being on her way to the airport and a new life.

Leaving her older half-sister to tidy up after her. It was now Alexa's job to clean up, apologise, explain.

That thought was enough to have Alexa's feet slowing as she moved away from where the car had just delivered her to the main door of the huge, elegant cathedral of Santa María de la Sede in the centre of Seville. Glancing upwards briefly, towards where the bell tower known as La Giralda was etched against the clear blue sky, she drew a deep, calming breath and squared her shoulders. At her back the crowd of paparazzi gathered to record the event called for her attention, and the flashing of cameras sounded like a fusillade of bullets, one she struggled to ignore as she climbed the couple of worn stone steps into the porch, her fingers reaching out for the heavy wrought-iron handle of the big, carved wooden door.

'You're not getting trapped that way, Nat. Not any more.'

She spoke the words out loud, shaking her head as she did so in an attempt to give them more emphasis, to make them mean more and have more effect. But even as she heard them she knew that they lacked the conviction she'd been aiming for. They weren't going to be able to give her the strength she needed to walk into the cathedral, announce what had happened and deal with the chaos that followed. And that was what she had to do. Because there was no one else.

'Come on, Alexa. You know you have to do this!'

Sighing with resignation, she accepted the truth as she forced herself forward again, curling her fingers around the big iron handle and gripping hard.

There was no one else who could sort this out. If she didn't do something then the whole dreadful, ugly mess would stay just as it was—in fact it would probably get so much worse. The explosion was going to be nuclear as it was. All she could hope to do was to try to contain some of the fallout so that the repercussions were at least manageable.

Nervousness made her palms damp so that her fingers slipped on the metal handle, foiling her first attempt to open the door.

'Oh, damn it!'

With nothing else available, she had no choice but to wipe her hands down the long skirt of her dress in an attempt to dry them off. The gesture did nothing for the appearance of the expensive pink satin, but then right now that was the least of her concerns. The ceremony that the dress had been planned for wasn't going to go ahead today after all, so it didn't matter at all what it looked like.

Besides, the dress wasn't really her style at all. It was the sort of glamorous look that her stepmother had chosen for the society wedding she had always hoped for for her daughter, and Alexa knew that the colour wasn't the most flattering for her dark brown hair and hazel eyes. But that had been all right when she had believed that the wedding was what Natalie wanted. It was Natalie's day and nothing was going to spoil her half-sister's wedding, even if it was to a man that Alexa felt was not right for her.

A wedding that was now no longer going to take place, Alexa reminded herself ruefully, reaching for the door handle again. She was going to need all her courage to go into the church and tell everyone that.

Her stepmother would probably have hysterics. Her father—and Natalie's—would become even stiffer, even more withdrawn, his mouth clamping tighter than ever before. And the groom...

And the groom...

The thought made a sensation like the frantic flutter of butterfly wings start to beat high up in Alexa's throat as the great door swung slowly open, to land with a hollow, sepulchral thud against the worn stone wall, the noise making everyone inside the church turn and stare in expectation.

She had no idea what the groom would say or do. No idea at all just how Santos Cordero would react to the news that his bride-to-be had jilted him at the altar, running away from her marriage and heading for the airport and another man. But just the thought made her shiver as her blood ran cold through her veins.

She had only met the man her half-sister was marrying once, at the family dinner in Santos's beautiful Moorish-style home just a few miles from Seville on the night of her arrival in Spain, two days before. But she'd heard so much about him. And she'd seen the effects that his influence had had on her father ever since the two men had embarked on a business deal together. It seemed now that every time she saw Stanley Montague he looked older, thinner, greyer. More shrunken somehow and clearly desperately stressed. Her dad was just not used to dealing with the financial sharks, and Santos Cordero was one of the biggest sharks of all.

Not for nothing was he known as *el Brigante*—the Brigand. A nickname that she had heard he lived up to in more ways than one.

'Just wait till you see him! He's such a hunk! And rich as sin,' Natalie had said, sounding so very enthusiastic.

Too enthusiastic, Alexa now realised, hearing in memory what she hadn't recognised then as the forced note in her sister's voice, betraying the careful effort Natalie had been making to sound like an excited young bride desperately in love with her husband-to-be.

But Natalie had been right about one thing at least—Santos was every bit as stunning as everyone had told her he would be. There was no denying that he was one of the most devastatingly handsome men she had ever met in her life. Tall, raven-haired, with a leanly powerful frame and powerfully carved features, he was a man for whom the description 'darkly dangerous' had to have been coined.

Hunk he might be, Alexa had told herself later when she had been introduced to Santos. But when she had come up close, close enough to shake his hand, close enough to look into his face, she had known intuitively that the 'dangerous' part of that description was not just fantasy or her imagination running riot.

His grip on her hand had been cool and firm, his careful smile polite and practised, but she had found herself looking

into the coldest, iciest eyes she had ever seen. A unexpectedly
pale grey gaze that seared over her with the cruel force of a
focused laser. Her skin had prickled all over and she had felt
alternately hot and then shiveringly cold as if she were in the
grip of some horrible fever. Murmuring some inane politeness, she had made her escape as soon as possible and from
then onwards had tried to avoid Santos for the rest of the
evening. But all the time she had felt the burn of his palm
against hers, and her body still tingled under the impact of that
scorching gaze.

'Alexandra?'

It was her father's voice, blurred and almost covered by the
murmurs of surprise from the congregation, coming to her
from where he had been waiting just inside the church—
waiting not for her but for his younger daughter to arrive.
Natalie had made the excuse that she didn't want to overtire
him, had insisted that her father went on ahead, rather than following tradition and travelling to the church in the same car
as the bride.

'Alexandra…'

'What has happened?'

Another voice sliced into the buzz of interest that had filled
the church with the realisation that the new arrival through the
door had been not the bride they were expecting but the chief
bridesmaid. A pale-faced, uncomfortable-looking bridesmaid
at that, Alexa reflected miserably as the cold, incisive tones of
the groom's question carried clearly down what seemed like
miles and miles of aisle and made every other conversation and
comment die away, like the tide ebbing back from the sand.

'What has happened?' he demanded again and unwillingly
Alexa's eyes went to where he stood at the altar, tall and
darkly, dangerously imposing.

If he had looked stunning in the sombre black and white
of the evening dress of the night of the party, so now, in the

formal morning coat, waistcoat and elegant cravat, he had an impact that made her head spin. And from the moment that her eyes clashed with his, green-brown locking with glittering grey, it was as if there were only the two of them in the world. The rest of the congregation, her surroundings, the flickering candles and the gorgeous flowers all merged into just one great blur, at the centre of which was a dark, strongly carved face, a tight, set mouth and burning, molten eyes.

'Tell me!' Santos Cordero said, and it was an autocratic command, flung at her with all the force of a perfectly aimed arrow, right from the far end of the church.

The impact of it flung her head back, bringing her chin up as her eyes flashed a defiance of his dictatorial tone and she watched his eyes narrow in swift assessment, his beautiful mouth tightening sharply.

'*Per favor,*' he added with such a bite and an obviously carefully controlled effort that it was like a slap in her face. Stinging hard.

It wasn't a 'please' at all, she thought furiously. It was just another way of phrasing a command, and in a tone that made her want to toss something rude at him and turn on her heel and march out. Either that or fling the shocking truth in his face and watch that arrogant glare fade from his face, the 'lord of all I survey' stance falter just a little so that his straight shoulders weren't held so high, the elegantly booted feet not planted quite so firmly on the stone-flagged floor of the church.

But even as the angry thoughts crossed her mind, a sense of decorum and a touch of unwilling compassion pushed them out again fast.

Arrogant brute though he might be, Santos Cordero was still a bridegroom on his wedding day. He had come here today believing he was going to be married to her half-sister, Natalie.

The same Natalie who had fled from her hotel and was

probably at the airport now with the man she had admitted she really loved.

Leaving it to her sister to explain just what was happening.

The thought dried her mouth, tightening her throat, and just for a moment she actually allowed herself the luxury of considering turning and running too, getting away from here as fast and as far as she could. This wasn't her problem; her responsibility. Let someone else explain to this arrogant Spaniard that his bride-to-be had had second thoughts. Let someone else...

There was no one else.

At the far end of the church, Alexa could see that her stepmother, resplendent in emerald-green and a hat with swirling peacock feathers, was twitching uncomfortably in her seat, her narrow face pale and taut as if she already suspected that something had gone very badly wrong. And her father...

No, she didn't dare to look into her father's face, knowing that he would guess she had brought the worst of news. And being her father he would probably erupt in a rage. Which could be the worst possible response right now.

'Señorita...'

Santos Cordero's pointed hint that she continue sounded gentle, but looking into his dark, set face, Alexa suddenly knew that gentle was the exact opposite of just what he was feeling. He had barely controlled his impatience, reining it in only with the most ferocious power. And even now it was very close to breaking free if the harshly drawn white lines about his nose and eyes, etched around that sexy mouth were anything to go by. Say the wrong thing and he would explode, the top blowing off his mental volcano and the red-hot lava of fury flowing out to engulf them with spectacularly nasty results if she wasn't very much mistaken.

This was the Santos Cordero she had been led to expect. This was *el brigante*, whose reputation for arrogance and ruthlessness had reached her even in Yorkshire, where her home was, miles away from the family house in London.

When her father had first announced that he was negotiating a business deal with Santos he had sounded so excited, totally confident that this partnership would make him a fortune and so ease all his financial problems. But it hadn't been long before everything had seemed to change. It was obvious that the deal was not the success Stanley had dreamed of but instead a source of great stress. Though just lately those worries seemed to have been buried in the unexpected rush to organise Natalie's wedding.

'*Señorita…*'

Once more those softly deadly tones drew her eyes to the face of the man her half-sister was supposed to have been marrying today. And once she had looked into those burning, deep-set eyes, even from this distance, she found it impossible to look away. She couldn't drag her own gaze from the mesmeric force of his and once more she had that shocking sense of tunnel vision. Of being at the far end of a long, long channel from where the only thing she could see was the tall, powerful form of Santos Cordero, every ounce of his attention totally focused on her.

'What is it that you have come here to say? Because you have come to say *something*, I assume?'

Drawing in her breath sharply, Alexa struggled to ignore the sting of that sarcastic tone, which had a bite like the flick of a whip.

'I have to speak to you,' she managed, the words coming out as breathlessly as if she had just run the couple of miles from her half-sister's hotel room to the cathedral. 'Please…' she added with renewed urgency when she saw the way that his black brows snapped together in a dangerous frown.

'Then speak.'

An autocratic flick of one long, bronzed hand emphasised the command with all the arrogance of a long-ago emperor.

'I for one am impatient to hear what you have to say.'

He was impatient all right. He couldn't make that any plainer. And she would tell him. But not right here, right now. Not like this with close on six hundred guests now openly gawping in her direction, fascinated by what was going on and anxious to view the next 'episode' in this soap-opera drama that had suddenly been staged before them.

With her heart beating so high up in her throat that breathing normally was a complete impossibility, she made herself take the necessary steps forward down the aisle that brought her near to him. And as she went she tested possible openings over and over inside her thoughts, trying each one for size and discarding them as too stupid, too contentious, too clumsy or just plain wrong. And even if she had any hope of an idea it fled from her mind in the moment that she looked up into his dark, shuttered face and saw the way those cold, hunter's eyes were burning down into her.

She knew that it wasn't possible but she suddenly felt that he was even bigger, leaner, stronger than he had appeared on the night she had been introduced to him. The formal tailoring of his wedding suit emphasised the straight width of his shoulders, the broad chest, narrow waist and long, long legs. And against the immaculate white of his shirt, the golden tones of his skin stood out in dramatic, powerful contrast.

'Can we go somewhere more private, please?'

Her voice was thin and uneven on the words but she knew that he had heard her even though he inclined his dark head to one side, frowned faintly, as if he had not quite caught what she had said.

'Perdon?'

He took a step forward as he spoke and she was close enough now to see the way the powerful chest rose and fell with his breathing, even see the faint shadow on his jaw where already the darkness of stubble was just visible below the surface. She almost believed she could actually feel the heat of his strong body reach out to enclose her, carrying with it the subtle tang of some citrusy cologne, enhanced and deepened by the clean, personal scent of his skin. Her heart was thudding even harder now, but this time she realised on a sense of shock that it was not just the sense of apprehension that gripped her but a sudden rush of a purely female response to the presence of a powerful, sexually alluring male. And that was the last thing she wanted to feel towards this man whose presence in their lives seemed to have created nothing but problems for her family.

'Can we go somewhere more private, please?'

She forced herself to say it again, more firmly and a touch louder this time, though she really wanted to hiss it at him in the most controlled of whispers, for his ears only.

'Somewhere we can be alone.'

'Alone?'

This time those black brows drew together with such sharp force that she almost heard the snap and it was impossible to misunderstand just what was in his mind. Alexa could feel the hot tide of blood race through her skin, heating it with embarrassment.

'*Señorita*, I am about to be married.'

'Not like that! I didn't mean it like that!' she hissed at him. 'And you're—'

With a sense of horror she choked off the appalling declaration—*you're not getting married*. She couldn't just come out and say it. Not like that. Just as she couldn't give him the devastating news right here and now, in front of this audience.

Because he had to be devastated, didn't he? Even if he was big and strong, and ruthless as they came, he had after all asked Natalie to marry him, to be his wife, for better, for worse...

'You really need to hear what I have to say,' she managed,

praying that the emphasis she was putting on the words hid the sudden huskiness that seemed to have affected her voice.

'*You* think I do.'

He was looking down his long, straight nose at her now, that broad forehead creased in a disapproving frown, silvery eyes darkened with frank disdain and total scepticism.

'You think I should hear what you have to say—but you give me no reason why you should march in here like this, without a word of explanation and demand that I—'

'I'm trying to explain!' Alexa snapped in total exasperation.

Couldn't he see that this was important? That she wouldn't have 'marched in here' like this if it weren't? Couldn't he see…?

No, she acknowledged to herself privately. He couldn't see at all. It was the last thing that would possibly cross his mind.

Of course *el brigante* would never consider that his bride might not turn up. That she might abandon her wedding, jilting her bridegroom and leaving him waiting at the altar. It would just never enter his handsome, arrogant head. Instead he had supreme confidence that she would be here, just as he had arranged, just as he wanted, and go ahead with the marriage—because he wanted it.

The immovable arrogance of the man was beginning to grate so much that she found she was actually clenching her teeth hard so as not to let rip with a furious and totally unvarnished declaration of the truth.

'But I think that you'd prefer it if we were alone to talk.'

'What I would *prefer* is not to be alone with an unknown woman just moments before my wedding ceremony. Can you imagine what the gutter Press would make of that?'

'Oh, if you're interested in preserving your reputation then you needn't worry! I can assure you that I have no designs on…'

Alexa's voice faded away as she caught the piercing, cynically sceptical look he slanted at her from those burning, silvery eyes. He really thought she was here as some sort of reputation-ruining exercise? What sort of life did this man lead that he had become so totally cynical, so appallingly suspicious? Did he truly believe that she would use the time they were alone together to blackmail him later—demanding a small fortune not to 'kiss and tell'?

Well, she had no intention of *kissing* at all…

That thought sent her unwary gaze flying to Santos's mouth, lingering just a moment too long on its sensual shape, the cynical half-smile curling the corners, and her heart skipped a beat. Kissing those lips would be an experience, one that set off flares of warning in her mind at just imagining it.

But 'Handsome is as handsome does,' as her mother was fond of quoting. And everything she had heard about Santos Cordero put that 'handsome does' part of the saying very much in doubt.

'I prefer not to know what designs you might have…'

The icy tones of the Spaniard's attractively accented voice dragged her thoughts back from the foolish path they were travelling, giving her a hint of perhaps one of the reasons why her half-sister had decided that she couldn't go through with this wedding.

'Oh, for heaven's sake, you impossible man,' she exploded. 'I'm trying to save you from embarrassment here.'

'Alexandra…'

It was her father who stepped forward, obviously determined to intervene, his face alternating between red and pale, his tone and his use of her full name a brusque reproach.

'Alexandra—please…'

But he stopped dead at a sudden lift of the Spaniard's hand, an autocratic signal to stop—stay away. Obviously something in what she had said had caught Santos Cordero's attention. That 'you impossible man,' Alexa strongly suspected. She doubted very much that he was regularly subjected to such a contemptuous description—if ever.

'If you're really afraid, then we can leave the door ajar so that someone will hear your screams when I...'

But no, she'd gone too far there. If she had meant to provoke him into a decision and action, then she had succeeded. More than succeeded. She had pushed him over some sort of edge that she hadn't even known was there and he had lost whatever remaining grip he had had on his tolerance, moving from an irritated, barely reined-in impatience in the blink of an eye. She could see it in the flash of cold fire in his eyes and in the way that his beautiful mouth thinned to a brutal, hard line.

And suddenly her heart was thudding in a very different way from the purely feminine response of just moments before. From being at least on secure ground, if not at all confident of her reception, she now felt as if the earth had shifted beneath her feet, opening up the stone flags to reveal a nasty, sucking, dragging swamp that was closing over her feet, starting to drag her in—drag her down.

Her throat was painfully dry and her thoughts spun as she slicked a nervous tongue over parched lips.

'Believe me, it really would be better if we spoke in private—in there perhaps...'

She waved an arm in a wild gesture towards a door that she presumed led to the church vestry.

Just what she was going to do if he dug in the heels of his highly polished handmade shoes and refused to go anywhere, she had no idea. But it seemed that she didn't even need to consider the possibility because from his obdurate refusal to co-operate, Santos now launched, suddenly and fast, into action. Swift as a striking snake, his hand came out and clamped hard fingers around her upper arm, their tips digging into the skin.

'You want to talk?'

His voice was harsh and thick with anger, his accent sounding strongly deep in his throat.

'Then we'll talk.'

And he marched her across to the arched wooden door that she had indicated, wrenching on the handle to push it open with scant ceremony. Bundling her inside, he kicked it closed behind him with equal disregard for both the church fitting and, obviously, the idea he had formerly held that being shut in a room with her might prove compromising.

Clearly that idea was long gone. In fact, to prove the point, he leaned back against the old, dark wood and folded his arms firmly across the width of his chest. If she had thought that his jaw was set, his mouth closed tight before, then it was nothing when compared with the hardness of his face now, the ruthless control of all but the single tight muscle that worked in his jaw.

'*Pues,*' he declared after a single flashing glance at the gold watch he wore on his left wrist. 'You have three minutes in which to explain just what all this is about—and believe me the explanation had better be good—otherwise…'

He let the threat trail off but all the same it still had enough force and note of danger in his tone to send an apprehensive shiver running down Alexa's spine.

'So? What do you have to say that is so important?'

'I…'

Twice she tried to get the words out and both times her voice failed her. Looking into his hard, set face was a mistake. It froze her throat around the words until she could hardly breathe. But looking away was no help either. How could you tell a man that the future he thought was his had been snatched away from him without looking him in the eye?

But looking him in the eye was quite beyond her.

'You've already wasted thirty seconds,' Santos gibed. 'Another couple of minutes and I will walk back out there and—'

'Natalie isn't coming!'

The words broke from her as any attempt at restraint or

control, or even coherence, was impossible. There wasn't a right way to say this, she told herself, not a good way and definitely not an easy way, so the only thing she could do was to fling the words out into the open and then hope to make a tactical withdrawal, flinching back out of the way of the fallout from the violent explosion that had to result when she made her announcement.

'Natalie isn't coming. She's changed her mind.'

Astonishingly the explosion she had been anticipating didn't come. But, if it was possible, the sudden dark and dangerous silence that greeted her outburst was actually worse. It was so long-drawn-out and so deep that she felt it take her nerves with it, stretching them out so painfully until she thought she might actually scream out loud with the tension.

'Changed her mind?' Santos finally echoed the words as if he couldn't believe what he had heard or if he did then he didn't understand just what it meant. 'Explain!' he rapped out, the cold command having the force of a bullet fired from a gun.

Well, he'd asked for it. She'd tried to be fair. She'd tried to be considerate. But it seemed that fair and considerate were concepts that Santos Cordero just didn't understand or appreciate.

'Natalie isn't coming to the wedding. She doesn't want to marry you after all.'

'Where…?' Another question was barked at her, the single syllable seeming to spark with anger in the air as it was flung from his lips. '*Where* the devil is my bride?'

Alexa would have sworn that it was impossible for his black brows to draw together any more sharply or for the burnished eyes to blaze any more furiously without smoke actually starting to fill the room, but somehow Santos managed to rein in his anger even though she could practically hear it crackling hot in his veins in contrast to the icy control of his beautifully accented voice.

'And why is she not here, at my side—before that altar, as she should be?'

'Oh, please!'

Alexa felt she couldn't take any more. His anger was one thing, when directed at her, but those words 'my bride' had almost destroyed her.

My *bride*. A word that should have meant the promise of love and joy and happily-ever-afters. But he made it sound so possessive.

'I'm sorry, but she's never going to be here, at your side, before that—that…'

The word eluded her overstressed brain and she could only manage a wild wave of her hand in the direction of the doorway against which he stood, meaning to indicate the church and the altar beyond it. The church where everyone— her family and his, his friends—were all still waiting for the wedding to begin. The wedding that would never begin now. Never take place.

'She's not coming. She's not going to marry you. She went to the airport but she'll be through to the departure lounge by now. She was taking a plane to America with the man she really loves. The man she really wants to marry.'

'She's gone.'

That icy precision was back in his voice, making her wince in sharp distress when she heard it. She had never felt quite so low and nasty as she did now, and it wasn't even her own battle she was fighting. But she couldn't have let Natalie go through with this marriage, the prospect of which was obviously making her so unhappy.

'Your sister—has run out on her wedding.'

There was a darkly dangerous note in his use of the word 'sister,' one that caught on something raw in Alexa's heart and twisted, cruelly, painfully. But she didn't dare to absorb the impact of it, take it out and look at it closely to see what it was really implying or what lay behind it. She didn't have time either. She'd finally almost managed to complete the mission that had brought her here. She'd told Santos the truth and she could now hope to leave, get out of here as fast as she could.

'She has jilted me—left me for some other man?'

'I'm afraid so.'

'She really should not have done that.'

'I know, and I am sorry—she should have told you before now, should have admitted to you that she didn't love you enough to marry you. I know you must be hurt—'

The tumbling words were starting to fall over each other, tangling together in her nervous haste, but they suddenly froze, shutting off completely in shock, as Santos's response broke into them.

And it was because it was not at all the response she expected that it caught her up short. In fact it was so much the opposite of the response she had been anticipating that she could only stand and stare, hazel eyes widening in stunned disbelief.

Because Santos had laughed.

When she had said that she understood how he must be hurting he had actually flung back his dark head, closed his silvery eyes briefly and laughed out loud. And it was not a pleasant laugh. It had nothing of any real humour in it, no warmth at all. It was a cold laugh, a harsh and bitter laugh, one that made a thousand tiny electrical shivers skitter over her skin and turn her veins to ice.

'Santos?' she queried, wondering if after all she had actually got through to him.

In her nervousness had she really made any sort of sense or had she just confused him? Was it possible that she had somehow made him think that this was some sort of joke—a very dark, sick one, but a joke none the less?

'Santos—did you hear what I said? You have to under-stand…'

'Oh, I heard, *belleza*, and I understand only too well. Your sister has reneged on her promise and run out on me, leaving you to pick up the pieces. That I understand only too well. What I do not get is why in hell you think I should care.'

CHAPTER TWO

'WHAT?'

Alexa found that she was blinking in confusion, trying to make sense of Santos's words, but most of all trying to understand or even believe in his reaction.

If that laugh had been unexpected, then the rest of his words sounded almost surreal. When she had been expecting distress, anger, bitterness at the way that he had been betrayed and left at the altar by the woman he wanted to marry, instead there was dark cynicism, and an almost careless dismissal of what she had just said.

'You don't care? But surely…?'

Santos's response was a shockingly indifferent shrug of his broad shoulders under the fine cloth of his immaculately tailored jacket, and he pushed both hands through the gleaming darkness of his hair as if relaxing after a long day.

But *relaxed* was the last word she would use to describe the set of his face, the tight compression of his sensual mouth, the way that a taut muscle jumped in his jaw. And the glittering look he turned on her had nothing that was comfortable or easy-going in it. Instead she was reminded of how, on the day she had first met him, she had believed that he had the coldest eyes of anyone in the world.

'You expect me to act as if your sister has broken my heart?

As if I have lost the love of my life and cannot find the strength to go on—to live for the future?' he questioned cynically, biting the words out as if they were bones he wanted to snap. 'Well, then you could not be more wrong. *I* will have no trouble going on with my life after this—though your family might find it harder to pick themselves up as a result. In fact—'

He broke off as a sharp rap came on the door, someone knocking on the heavy panels from the other side, in the church.

'Alexandra? Alexa?'

It was her father's voice, coming sharp and concerned through the thickness of the wood.

'Is everything all right? What's going on? Cordero—what—'

'*Momento!*' Santos snapped, tossing the word over his shoulder, his burning eyes still fixed on Alexa's bewildered face. 'We will be out in a second and then we will explain all. Or rather…'

The cold, curt tone slid into something else as his eyes seared across her skin, seeming to strip away a necessary protective layer and leave her nerves raw and exposed underneath.

'*You* will do the explaining,' he said and for all the sudden softness and smoothness of his tone Alexa could be in no doubt that it was an autocratic command, one that he expected to have obeyed without hesitation or argument. 'You will tell your father—your family—what has happened.'

'But I…' Alexa began, her voice failing her, the words drying in her throat as she tried to protest. 'It isn't up to me now—surely you…'

She couldn't go out there and tell everyone why she was here. Tell them that Natalie had run out on her wedding—the wedding that had been described in the newspapers and the gossip columns as the Wedding of the Year, the joining together of huge wealth and aristocratic beauty. It was to have been the union of one powerful rich, ultra modern bloodline of the billionaire entrepreneur, and the old, patrician lineage of Natalie Montague, twenty-year-old daughter of Lord Stanley Montague. Santos Cordero who had made his fortune with his own hands and brain, dragging himself up from his lowly and impoverished beginnings to the height of his wealth and power, was marrying into the British nobility, a family whose name had been amongst the highest in the land for centuries past. It had been the stuff that fairy tales were made of, especially when the bride was acknowledged to be a stunning beauty and the groom a hunk whose carved, handsome features and lean, powerful frame had featured in many photographs in the gossip columns and in magazines, usually with some supremely decorative female draped on his arm.

'I don't think...' she tried again, feeling even more lost and adrift than in the first moments when she had arrived in the church and had come under the scrutiny of those coldly burning eyes as she walked up the aisle towards him.

Because the truth was that she didn't know what she was meant to say or how—and what—she was supposed to explain. Nothing had been as she had expected it. But then how did you know what might happen when you had to break up a wedding by announcing to the groom that his fiancée had jilted him? It wasn't exactly something that you did every day.

But Santos wasn't listening to her protests. Instead he had levered himself away from the door and taken two swift strides towards her, his hand coming out and clamping over her arm, just above the elbow, hard fingers digging into her skin as he swung her round to face the door at his side.

'*You* will do it,' he declared, cold and brusque. 'Your family has messed up my life enough already, so now...'

He was interrupted by another rap at the door and her father's voice again, sharper this time.

'Alexandra—what's going on in there...?'

'Nothing—I mean, it's fine,' Alexa managed when Santos turned a forceful glare on her, the burnished eyes directing a silent command that she should respond. 'We—we're coming out now and I'll…I'll explain.'

She had no option, it seemed, because that hand that gripped her arm was now pulling her forward, leaving her no choice but to follow.

'Let go of me!' she spat in furious protest. 'OK, so I had to bring you bad news—but there's a saying about not shooting the messenger. And that's all that I am—the messenger. Natalie's the one—'

'But your sister is not here.'

It was a low growl and he didn't look at her, didn't slow his steps towards the door, yanking it open as soon as he reached it.

'So don't take it out on me! You can't drag me about like this—'

She'd taken her attention off her own feet for a moment and as a result she caught her toe against one of the uneven flagstones, stumbling awkwardly in the unaccustomed high-heeled shoes. For a second she thought she would fall but then that cruel grip around her arm tightened even more, holding her upright by sheer force.

'Don't yank me about!'

'I was trying to help.'

The cold flash of his brilliant eyes warned her not to argue but her own temper was bubbling up sharply and she was having to struggle to contain it. How had this happened? How had she come from being just, as she had said, the messenger of bad news, to being the victim of Santos Cordero's dark disapproval, hauled out into the church by him to face the congregation assembled for his society wedding, without even being aware of just what was involved?

Because something was involved, that much was obvious.

'Then don't *help*.' She laced her tone with sarcasm to make it clear that helping was the last thing she thought he was doing. 'I can manage quite well enough on my own.'

'You might be able to manage,' he flung back from between gritted teeth, keeping his voice low so that no one, not even her stepmother in the front row, or her father, still waiting by the altar steps, could catch what he was saying. 'But I would prefer it if you didn't fall flat on your face and then blame it on me. And I want to make sure that you don't take off like your sister and disappear out the door.'

'What would it matter if I did?'

For a second Alexa was tempted to aim a hard, pointed kick at Santos's ankle but another of those flashing sidelong glances seemed to catch her intent and a grim smile crossed his mouth as he brought them both to a halt right in front of the altar.

'Alexa,' her father began once more but silenced himself hastily when Santos turned a burning glare on him.

'Ladies and gentlemen…'

He barely had to raise his voice to be heard, the church had fallen so silent as soon as they had appeared. Every eye in the place was fixed on them, some faces frowning in confusion and puzzlement, others, like those of her father and step-mother, looking pale and taut with tension. Just what was going on here? What were the undercurrents she was just not picking up on? The things she didn't understand?

But Santos didn't seem to be aware of them as he continued to speak as calmly and as confidently as if he were making his after-dinner speech—the one that now would never have to be made.

'There has been a slight change of plan…'

Slight?

That brought Alexa's head round to his in a reaction of stunned shock. How could he describe Natalie's jilting of him, her flight to the airport, as a 'slight change of plan'?

But Santos ignored her total consternation, her wide, shocked eyes and continued with total control.

'The wedding is not going to take place.'

'Not…'

The word was choked from her father as he took an unsteady step backwards. And in the front pew, Alexa saw how her stepmother went even whiter, one expensively manicured hand flying to her mouth as if to hold back the cry of shock and disbelief that almost escaped her.

'What…?'

It was Stanley Montague, trying again to make his tongue work, to ask the question that was so obviously whirling round and round in his head. Alexa had rarely seen her father looking so shocked and upset. In fact, his reaction seemed out of all proportion to the situation. OK, so it was bad, there was going to be a terrible embarrassment to face, and the aborted wedding would be the talk of their friends—and probably the gossip columns for some weeks to come.

But surely that was better than Natalie making a huge mistake and marrying a man she didn't love? Better to call the wedding off now than to face a costly divorce—costly in more ways than financial—maybe just months from now? But her father was looking as if the end of the world had come and…

Alexa had no chance to think things through further because at that moment Santos's firm grip on her arm propelled her forward so that she was standing just in front of him, facing the gaping congregation.

'Natalie is not coming,' he said coolly. 'She has run out on me—that is what her sister came here to tell me. And now she's going to explain it all to you.'

A forceful little push made her take another step forward in the same moment that it pointedly told her that now was the time for her to speak—to tell everyone the truth.

But what *was* the truth? Suddenly Alexa was not quite sure. She only knew that it had been obvious that Natalie didn't want to go through with the wedding. But why had she ever agreed to it in the first place? That question made the

earth seem to shift beneath her feet. But she didn't have time
to consider the possible implications of that before her father
found his voice.

'Alexandra? What is happening?'

'Tell him,' Santos prompted harshly when she still hesitated. 'Tell them.'

'I'm afraid San—Señor Cordero is right…'

The way that her words echoed round the silent church
had an eerie, hollow sound but at least her voice had more
strength than she had anticipated and she sounded as if she
knew what she was talking about. How far that was from the
truth only she knew.

'Natalie has changed her mind. She doesn't feel it would
be right to marry him. Not when she realises that she truly
loves someone else.'

And that at least she could say with conviction. In her mind
she still had a clear image of the moment that she had looked
into her sister's hotel room and seen Natalie sitting on the bed,
staring at the beautiful wedding dress that hung in the
wardrobe, her face pale and drawn, her eyes flooded with tears.

'I thought I could do this, Lexa,' her sister had said. 'I really
wanted to—but it just isn't going to work now. If John hadn't
come into my life I would have gone ahead…but he did…and
meeting him has changed everything.'

'She's truly sorry to have messed everyone about…but she
knew it was better to break it off now than to go into a
marriage that she knew wasn't really right for her—'

'And she did not have the courage to come and tell me
herself?'

It was Santos who spoke, his low, darkly dangerous tone
drawing her eyes to his face. The black fury that blazed in
those eyes, the bitter, insulted pride that tightened his jaw,
turned his mouth to a thin, hard line, sent a shiver down her
spine as his hard, unyielding gaze locked with hers. Privately

she acknowledged that she couldn't blame Natalie for not wanting to face him. When he looked like this she couldn't imagine why her sister would ever have wanted to marry him in the first place.

'No,' she managed uncomfortably. Natalie hadn't even dared to face her mother and father with the truth. 'I'm sorry.'

If the slight inclination of his proud head was meant to be an acknowledgement of her apology then it failed to have any impact. There was no lightening of the coldness of his eyes, no easing of the tightness of every muscle in his powerful frame. And to think that she had once worried that the news of Natalie's flight might *hurt* him!

This man looked as if nothing could touch him. As if nothing could penetrate that armoured hide and reach through to find his heart. Right now he didn't even look as if he had a heart to touch.

'So where is Natalie now?'

Another question from her father drew Alexa's attention back to where Stanley was standing, hands clenched tightly together, a frown creasing his forehead.

'On her way to the airport—no…'

A quick glance at her watch confirmed her suspicion.

'She must be through to Departures by now. She was getting a plane…'

'Oh, no! Natalie!'

It was Petra Montague, Stanley's second wife, reacting in exactly the way that Alexa had anticipated that her stepmother would. Her narrow hands had come up before her face, fluttering weakly against her sculpted cheeks. Above the long, dark red nails her wide blue eyes appeared to glisten with tears that she was fighting not to shed.

'What has she done? What will we do?'

'Hush, my dear.' Stanley's response sounded almost like a reproach rather than an attempt at consolation as he stepped forward to take his wife's hands in his and hold them tightly, looking deep into her glistening eyes.

'Petra—don't…'

Alexa took a couple of steps forward, then stopped, knowing that her stepmother would not want her attempts at comfort. In fact, she would probably repulse them as dramatically as she was now clinging to her husband's hands and gazing up forlornly into his eyes.

'Surely it's better this way than for her to realise later that she's made a terrible mistake,' she repeated.

Oh, she was good, Santos told himself, watching the way Alexa had moved forward then hesitated, noting the quiet, soothing note of her voice. Listening to her, watching her, he could almost believe that she was genuine. That she believed every last word of the story that had dropped so convincingly from her pretty mouth.

But of course that couldn't be true. She had to be in this right up to her elegant neck. She must have known that her sister was going to run out on him; why else would she time her arrival at the church so perfectly that it was impossible for anyone to go after Natalie and bring her back?

They were all in it together—the whole family. And he had been foolish enough to let them persuade him to let his guard down and, for the first time in his life, make a bad decision.

As a wedding present for your bride… He could still hear Petra Montague's beseeching voice inside his head. *You wouldn't want to see your father-in-law thrown out into the street…*

Dios! What had he been thinking? Never before had he paid out anything on a contract before the whole deal was signed and sealed, but this time he'd let his guard slip just a centimetre and the damn Montague family had taken full advantage of it.

'You must want Natalie to be happy.'

'She would have been happy with Santos!' Petra wailed. 'We would all have been happy with things that way!'

'But she *wasn't* happy,' Alexa protested. 'She just didn't dare say it, once the wedding had been arranged and everything planned.'

From where he stood slightly to the side, all that Santos could see was this Alexa's face and body in profile, and, having looked at her once, he suddenly found it impossible to look away.

'Plain' was the way her stepmother had described her. 'Dull and old-fashioned'. But even at the pre-wedding party he had not seen her in that way. She didn't have Natalie's dramatic colouring, her stunning beauty. In the older girl, everything was toned down, her sister's blonde hair subdued to a dark brown, and no blue, blue eyes but an unusual hazel of the sort that could be green or brown depending on the light and her mood. And her clothes had been so much simpler than her sister's, more demure than Natalie's ultra-fashionable style, perhaps, but not 'dull' or old-fashioned.

Now, even under the appallingly unflattering and over-elaborate hairstyle, her profile had a purity that caught the eye and held it. Her skin was so pale it was almost translucent and the length of the lush, curling eyelashes that rested on her cheeks as she looked down seemed almost as if they might waft a breeze across the church with each movement of her eyes.

Her figure was tall and slender, slight in comparison to her sister's voluptuous curves, but she held herself with a natural elegance. She might not be as stunning a beauty as her sister but there was something about her that drew his attention to her.

Something that hooked him and held him watching, caught by her stillness, her composure. Something that intrigued him and wouldn't let him go.

On the day they had met she had been so cool, so distant, the ice maiden personified, that he had disliked her on sight. She had turned those hazel eyes on him in the sort of look that he had seen too often as he was growing up. The expression that reminded him he had clawed his way out of the gutter and that he still carried the taint of the slums along with him. It was a look that he had vowed he would never let anyone subject him to ever again and, seeing it, he had told himself that if he had had to choose then he would have preferred Natalie to this cold, stiff, unwelcoming woman.

Now he was no longer so certain.

'But one thing's for sure,' she was saying now, the calm, soft tones of her voice carrying clearly even above her step-mother's near-hysterics, her father's attempts at soothing. 'I'm afraid there isn't going to be a wedding here today. I just couldn't let Natalie go through with it.'

Couldn't... The word swung round and round in Santos's head, sending warning echoes out like the ripples in a pond when a pebble was thrown into it. *I just couldn't let Natalie go through with it.*

Couldn't, be damned. She had been part of this all along. She'd known that Natalie was going to break her promise, had helped her run out on the wedding.

Helped her humiliate him in this public way.

'I'm sorry that you've all had a wasted journey, but I'm sure you'll understand. And now I suppose the only thing we can do is to go home and get on with our lives.'

She was moving forward as she spoke, making it plain that she was about to do just that, about to walk down the aisle, out of the church...

'So if you'd all like to leave...'

'No!'

That was not going to happen. She wasn't going to just walk away from this, walk out on the mess she and her family had created, and leave it all behind without a backward look. The furious feeling that he had been duped and robbed was like a blaze in his mind, obliterating rational thought, driving him into action. His hand shot out and fastened around her arm again, pulling her to a halt with such force that she actually spun round again, coming face to face with him. Natalie might be beyond his reach, but her sister was not.

The Montague family owed—and he didn't care who started paying. Only that someone did. And this other daughter seemed a good place to start.

But first he had to make sure that she didn't get away from him now, running out on him fast like her deceitful, lying little sister.

'No,' he repeated even more forcefully. 'You are not going anywhere—you are coming with me.'

'Why?'

Once again Alexa was strongly tempted by the idea of a swift kick on the ankle bone of the haughty, autocratic male who held her captive as he glared down into her face, just inches away from his. Only the thought of the audience still seated in the pews behind them kept her from actually physically attacking him, though she glared up into his arrogantly handsome face, praying that her defiance and determination showed in her own eyes as they locked with his.

'Why on earth would I want to go anywhere with you?'

'Because I am asking you to,' Santos said with a swift, totally unexpected smile.

The transformation in his face was so sudden, so astonishing that it made her blink in total disbelief. From being coldly tyrannical and domineering, he had suddenly switched to deliberate and persuasive charm.

And it was working, she admitted unwillingly to herself as she felt the unexpected change in her pulse rate, the new unevenness of her heartbeat in response to the softening of his expression, that stunning smile. She didn't want to feel that she was weak enough to respond to the practised charm of an experienced male seducer, but the truth was that she couldn't stop herself. When that smile curved the sensual lips and the light illuminated his burnished eyes, then she suddenly found some of the prickly defensiveness with which she had confronted him melting away and being replaced by an intensely feminine and totally instinctive response.

'Look…'

The way he raised his voice, the swift gesture of his hand towards the congregation was a move to include everyone in what he was saying. But the direction of his eyes, the burn of their focus was meant for her and for her alone. And the sheer force of it knocked her off balance before she had a chance to collect herself, win back her much needed control.

'The wedding may have to be cancelled—this part of things spoiled—but does the whole of the day have to be ruined? I have a reception prepared back at my home. My staff and the caterers have been working for days to get things ready. It would be a crime to let everything go to waste.'

For a moment longer he held her gaze and the searing intensity of his eyes made her head spin with the message it seemed to be giving before he suddenly glanced up again, looking out at their audience and switching on another of those impossible, seductive smiles.

'As Señorita Montague says, so many of you have had a long journey here. What sort of a host would I be if I let you leave again without any refreshment, anything to eat? I invite you all back to the house. There might no longer be any need for a wedding reception but I hope you will enjoy my hospitality just the same.'

Alexa could scarcely believe what she was hearing. She knew that just a few minutes before, there, in the little room just off the altar, he had asked her why he should care that his bride had jilted him at the altar. But could he really just turn and walk away from what was supposed to have been his wedding—and invite all his guests along to share in the abandoned reception?

The cold-eyed man she had first met might be able to. But would the man with the lethally charming smile she had just seen? And which one of them was the real Santos Cordero?

'You—you won't want us there…' she managed. 'The Montague family would be the last people you'd want to come along. The spectres at the feast, as it were…'

Her voice trailed off again as once more she was treated to that brilliant, enticing smile, but one that she felt was touched with an iciness that was infinitely disturbing.

'On the contrary, you are more than welcome.'

Was she fooling herself or had there been a deliberate emphasis on that *you*? Surely he couldn't mean just her?

'I am sure that you will want to help me get through this time that I should have been spending with my new bride.'

Now that had very definitely been laced with something darker, more ominous, the hint of a threat that made her skin crawl in uncomfortable response.

'I think not…' Alexa tried but Santos ignored her and swept on as if she hadn't even attempted to speak.

'And I am sure that your stepmother would prefer to have somewhere to regain her composure before she has to face the paparazzi.'

'The paparazzi?'

She hadn't thought about that. The truth was that she hadn't been able to think beyond the actual delivery of her sister's message. After that, her imagination hadn't been able to stretch to consider the possibilities.

'But of course.'

This time Santos's smile was pure ice; nothing charming or even pleasant about it at all. It was a smile that destroyed all the warmth that had filled her just moments before, leaving her feeling drained and lost and suddenly very fearful for the future, though for no reasons she could put her finger on.

'You don't think that they will let a scoop like this pass

them by without comment? The wedding of the year turning into the non-event of the year. It will be just the sort of thing they'd love to report. And they'll tear your family to pieces to get it.'

The pale grey eyes slid to where Petra was still wailing her distress on the front pew, with Stanley struggling to soothe her but actually looking as pale and worried as his wife himself. Once more Alexa shivered as she felt that sensation like something cold and slimy crawling over her skin. She could just imagine how her stepmother would go to pieces in front of the cameras, the pictures that would appear in the gossip columns the next day.

'And you could stop that?'

'I have men employed to make sure that the Press don't get too close. And I have a fleet of cars waiting to take everyone from the church to the reception.'

Alexa nodded silently. She'd travelled to the church in one of those cars. Big, sleek limousines with smoked-glass windows that provided the occupants with efficient protection from the flash of camera lights, the prying lenses. And she'd seen the efficient security that had ringed the cathedral, making sure that no one who wasn't on the guest list could get through.

'Why would you do that—for us?'

'Obviously I have my own reasons for not wanting the story of what has happened here today plastered all over the scandal sheets. Once inside my home, we can all relax.'

Relax. The word had so much appeal to it. Alexa's whole body was starting to ache as if she had been holding herself tense for so long that she had forgotten how it had felt to be any other way. Every muscle was tired and her head was starting to pound.

'Then thank you. I'll tell my father—get him and Petra into a car.'

'No. Miguel will see to that.'

One hand lifted in a silent signal to someone at the back of the church in the same moment that Santos moved once more to hold her back. But this time his powerful fingers laced with hers, closing tight over her hand as he restrained her. Alexa's heart jumped painfully as she felt the warmth of his palm curve against hers, heating her blood and sending it pulsing up her arm towards her heart. Her fingers tingled, her skin felt scorched and her mouth seemed to dry suddenly in the heat so that she slicked her tongue over parched lips to ease the sensation.

He had moved closer too and the scent of his body seemed to surround her like a warm mist, tangy with some light cologne overlaid by the muskier, more intimate aroma of his skin. Just inhaling it set all the tiny hairs on the back of her neck lifting in sensitive response, and her heart thudded even harder, forcing her to snatch in a swift, sharp, much needed breath of air.

'You will come with me.'

It was a command, not a suggestion. The tone of his voice said that he wouldn't listen to any argument, and the way that his hold on her hand tightened meant that she could not pull away as he headed away from the altar, dragging her with him.

She should be worried—probably even a bit frightened, Alexa admitted to herself as she trotted in his wake, trying to keep up with the long, powerful strides that took him down the aisle at a pace she couldn't quite manage. And she was just a bit of both.

But right at this moment, discretion very definitely seemed the better part of valour in this situation. Digging in her heels, refusing to move, would only cause another, bigger scene, and she had already had more than enough stress and emotional tension for one day.

In one thing at least, Santos was right. With the paparazzi

baying at the door of the church, they would soon suspect that something was wrong when they realised that the bride was not going to turn up, and then they were going to have a field day. The sooner everyone got out of here the better.

The journey back to Santos's elegant mansion would only take a few minutes, and once there she would be able to escape, lose herself in the crowd of guests, the force of his presence diluted by the presence of so many others.

Surely the worst was over and things could only get easier from now on?

CHAPTER THREE

HAD SHE REALLY thought that things would get easier? Alexa asked herself a couple of hours later. The truth was that she really had no idea whether things were getting better—or so much worse.

Restless and totally ill at ease, Alexa prowled around the huge blue and gold dining room in which the meal that was to have been part of the reception following Santos Cordero's wedding had been served and where now a small army of his staff was clearing away the remains of the wonderful food.

It had been delicious, at least, the one or two mouthfuls she had tried had been out of this world, but she had found it impossible to actually swallow more than a couple of bites. Her stomach had been churning so wildly, her head throbbing, and a feeling as if a hundred thousand butterflies were dancing along her veins had made it almost impossible to try and sit still.

And matters had been made so much worse by the way that Santos had insisted that she sit beside him. Right next to him in the seat that should have been his bride's place. Instead of which it had been his bride's sister who had taken that seat, looking totally out of place in the unaccustomed finery of her bridesmaid's dress, with her hair already starting to escape from the over-elaborate style that Petra had insisted on...

'What *am* I doing here?' Alexa murmured to herself as she

paused by one of the huge French windows that opened out onto a wide stone balcony overlooking the huge grounds, staring out at the sweeping slope that led to the woods on one side and the enormous rectangular swimming pool on the other.

Right now the blue water sparkled beautifully in the sun, making her think longingly of pulling off her clothes and plunging into its cool depths. Or at the very least kicking off the elegant shoes that were crippling her and dangling her feet over the edge, letting the water ease the aches and the raw spots where the narrow straps had rubbed too much.

'So this is where you're hiding yourself...'

The deep, accented male voice pulled her out of her reflections, bringing her back into reality in the space of a heartbeat. She had only heard—what?—a few thousand words spoken in that voice this afternoon on top of little more than a hundred on the night they had first met, but she knew that for ever onwards she would always recognise it, only needing to hear a couple of syllables in that rich, deep timbre, that sexy accent, and she would know instantly who was behind her.

'I'm not hiding. After all, nobody wants to see me. Just taking a breather.'

Deliberately she kept her gaze fixed on the scene beyond the window. She didn't want to look into Santos's face, knowing that would only scramble the thoughts that she was fighting so hard to clear. Besides, she had faced him all the way here, studied that shockingly handsome face close up, tried to read just what was going on behind those amazing eyes, the lush black lashes, tried to judge his mood from the tone of every word he spoke—and she had failed miserably. Whatever was going on in his mind, he was hiding it from her without any effort. Everything he said, every gesture, every expression that crossed his face gave away nothing at all.

'And trying to work out what the hell I'm doing here.'

'You're here as my guest—like everyone else.'

'A guest at a reception for a wedding that never was. It seems a weird thing to be celebrating.'

'You don't think that it's a practical solution to a possible problem? I had no intention of wasting the money I'd paid out for this.'

'You paid for the reception?' It had confused her from the start. She had wondered too why the marriage was to take place in Spain, but Natalie had said that Santos had insisted on it. 'But why?'

'Your father could not afford to do things the way that your stepmother wanted—I could.'

It was blunt and matter-of-fact, but surprisingly without the note of dark cynicism she might have expected. And somehow that worried her more. She knew that her stepmother had extravagant tastes, and it had been obvious lately that her father was struggling to indulge her in the way he had once done.

'And I intended that my bride should have only the best.'

Which was a stiletto-sharp dig that made her wince. Santos might have declared that he didn't give a damn that Natalie had walked out on him, and yet he was a man who had been prepared to spend heavily to make sure that she had a wedding day to be proud of. It didn't quite add up.

'You've been very generous.'

Santos shrugged off her attempt at thanks.

'If I had not invited everyone back here, I would have been overwhelmed with expensive food and wine with no one to help me deal with it. And not everyone ate as little as you did.'

So he had noticed the way that she had simply pushed her food around on her plate and hadn't been able to force herself to choke much of it down. The feeling of having been watched so closely, of his noting everything she did, was unnerving, making her shift uneasily from one foot to the other.

Behind her, his tall, powerful figure was reflected in the glass of the window as evening darkened the grounds, and, in spite of the fact that in her three inch heels she almost matched him in height, she still felt that he dwarfed her, towering over her where she stood. He had discarded his elegant jacket and the cutaway armholes of the silk waistcoat emphasised the power of his arms, the width of the broad, straight shoulders.

'Was the food not to your taste?'

'It wasn't that, I didn't like the feeling of being watched—being on show. I felt as if everyone was staring—wondering just why I was there.'

'Who gives a damn what anyone else thinks?'

Not him, obviously, his tone said.

She couldn't continue this conversation without looking at him and so she forced herself to spin round on her heel until she was facing him, looking up into that dark, stunning face.

Not that it helped her in any way. If she had thought that his expression was closed and shuttered against her in the car on the journey here when he had hardly spoken a single word all the way, then it was even more sealed off from her now.

Anyone watching them would simply see polite attention, the natural courtesy of a considerate host to one of his guests, stamped onto the beautifully carved profile, faintly curving the beautiful shape of his sensual mouth. But facing him head-on, Alexa couldn't be unaware of the total control he was imposing over every feature, every expression.

His eyes were so hooded they were almost half-closed, giving him a sleepily sensual look that had the most devastating effect on her heart rate, making it thud slow and heavy until she heard its echoes deep inside her head. But beneath those heavy lids, sleepy was the last thing the burnished eyes actually were. They gleamed with sharp intent as he watched each move she made, followed every tiny gesture, every revealing twitch of a muscle.

'And you needed to avoid the paparazzi,' Santos continued. 'I gave you a way to do that.'

'I'm grateful…'

Her voice shook slightly with the memory of the pack of reporters who had been waiting outside the church, as close to the grounds as the heavy ring of security would let them get. Shielded by Santos's large frame, hurried into the sleek limousine, hidden behind the smoked-glass windows, she had still been aware of the size of the crowd, the loud buzz of interest, the shouted questions. The cameras had flashed wildly too until she had felt as if she were in the middle of some dramatic firework display and she huddled in the back of the car, cowering away from the windows.

'And so, I'm sure, are my father and stepmother.'

She'd only seen them once since they had arrived at Santos's beautiful home. Her father had been supporting her mother, helping her into a seat, fetching her a brandy, though the truth was that he looked fit to drop himself. Natalie's defection had hit them both hard and for that reason she had to be grateful to Santos for the way he had taken action.

'Protecting us from the Press might have been the start to it but there was more to it than that.'

'You think so?'

The lift of an arching black brow questioned her statement, sending a rush of hot blood into her face. She always felt as if she was on the wrong foot with this man. From the moment that she had arrived at the church to tell him that the wedding was off, he had never once reacted in the way that she had anticipated. Once again she felt as if the ground beneath her feet was shifting dangerously.

What makes you think that you matter enough for that? the look in his eyes said.

'Well, there has to be more, or none of this makes any sense.'

'You're here because I want you here,' Santos inserted smoothly. 'And that is all that matters.'

'And you always get what you want?'

He didn't actually answer her question verbally. He didn't have to. The look in his eyes, the slight inclination of his head, told her all that she needed to know. But the dangerous thing was the reaction that she couldn't quite control. The sudden fizz of excitement that bubbled up inside her at his words. The quiver of delight at the thought that he would actually describe her as someone he wanted here with him. Someone for whom he was prepared to scheme and manoeuvre in order to get her into his home.

Things like that didn't happen to her. Men like Santos didn't happen to her... Not to home-loving librarians with no figure to speak of and mousy, ruler-straight hair. They happened to girls like Natalie. To petite, blonde-bombshell party girls with stunning figures and blue, blue eyes.

'You seem to have recovered remarkably well,' she declared suddenly, needing to cover her own confusion with a challenge that sounded overly aggressive because of the uncomfortable thoughts behind it. 'I can't imagine anyone else who has so recently been jilted at the altar being such an affable host.'

'You'd expect me to have collapsed on the church steps, weeping?' Santos enquired sardonically. The flashing look from those brilliant eyes told her just how far off the mark she was if she did.

'But if you wanted to marry her—if you loved her...'

'Love?'

It was a sharp, cynical laugh, one that was so cold and mocking that it made Alexa flinch back against the wall, away from its savagery.

'I don't believe in love. Never have. Never will.'

'Then why were you going to marry Natalie?'

This time his eyes narrowed so sharply that they were just glinting slits in his face, a dark frown drawing his black brows together. Alexa suddenly had the uncomfortable feeling that she was like some small, defenceless butterfly, laid out on a microscope slide, ready for dissection.

'It was what your sister wanted. She wanted it and it suited me. There was nothing like love involved.'

'You were going to marry my sister just…' Alexa began angrily but then the words faded from her tongue as she fully registered the impact of the second thing he had said. 'No…she wouldn't!'

She shook her head so violently that another few strands of her hair escaped from the pins securing them in ornate curls on her scalp and flew out around her head.

'Why so indignant, *belleza*?' Santos questioned softly. 'Surely you knew?'

'Well, yes…'

Natalie had admitted that she didn't love Santos, and now he had made it plain that he hadn't loved her either— so what had her sister been planning to be? Merely a trophy wife? Was even *el brigante* capable of such cold-blooded machinations?

Santos caught hold of her chin in hard fingers and held it, stilling her uneasy movement. The way he tilted her face up to his forced her to look deep into his eyes. Locking with the darkened gaze that burned down into hers.

'Why does that shock you so much? Many people marry for convenience—for dynastic reasons.'

'Older families, maybe—in other countries. Or people who need the money. But not people like you—you don't…'

Horrified, she caught herself up sharply, almost biting down on her tongue in her haste to have the foolish, revealing words silenced. What was she thinking of? What had she come so very close to saying—and so giving herself away?

'People like me don't what?' Santos asked, the very softness of the question revealing just how dangerous it really was. 'What were you about to say, Alexa—hmm?'

'Well—you don't need any money, do you? You're rolling in the stuff—disgustingly so.'

That made those heavy, arched brows shoot up in a way that made her stomach twist uncomfortably. She knew she had spoken rashly, over-emphatically, but she had been trying to conceal the true path her thoughts were following, which was that a man like Santos, someone who was so stunningly good-looking, so wealthy, so successful, would never need to buy a wife or to enter into any sort of a marriage of convenience. He would only have to crook his little finger and women would be lining up outside his door.

And would she be one of them? Her mind skittered away from even considering that question, never mind answering it. It was just too risky to what little was left of her composure.

'Disgustingly?' Santos echoed, an odd note creeping into his voice. 'You don't approve of my wealth?'

'Not when you use it to take over other people's lives.'

'Your sister was not "taken over…"'

Folding his arms across his broad chest, Santos leaned back against the wall and subjected her to a slow, sweeping survey, the narrowed eyes moving from the top of her head right down to where her feet still ached inside the tight, elegant shoes. Lingering for a second, his gaze then swept swiftly back up to her face and the flame in his eyes was not one of appreciation but a cold, burning anger that made her flinch deep inside.

'She knew very well what she was going to get out of it.'

And perhaps, at first, that had seemed enough, Alexa acknowledged. Thinking back over the way that Natalie had looked, the things she'd said, she had to admit that Nat had been excited by the idea of marrying Santos—at least at the beginning. She'd loved being seen on his arm, appearing in all the gossip magazines. It was only later, when she'd met this new man, that things had changed.

'And what about you? What did you get out of it?'

'I wanted a wife. Legal heirs to inherit all I've worked for.'

'There are other ways…'

This time the flashing glance that seared over her practically sizzled with contempt. She couldn't have said anything more stupid, anything he would believe in less, his expression said.

'If you're thinking love and romance and happily ever after then forget it. I told you, I don't believe in love.'

'Why not?'

'It does not exist.'

It was the coldest, most definite statement possible and one that left her in no possible doubt that she would be foolish to try and argue him out of his stance. She might as well bang her head hard against the stone wall that surrounded the terrace, leading to the curving steps down to the swimming pool. But she was so appalled at the black cynicism of his tone, the opaque appearance of his eyes, as if he had shut himself off from her, that shock and disbelief pushed unthinking words from her mouth.

'And so you bought yourself a wife.'

'No,' Santos drawled cynically. 'I did not buy…'

'What else would you call it?'

'I would not call it anything, *señorita*. Nothing at all. Because, if you remember, I did not end up with a wife at all. My fiancée did not keep her promise.'

The pointed reminder was guaranteed to close Alexa's throat completely, choking off any words she might have managed. He was right, of course, whatever their arrangement had been, Natalie had broken her promise to him. A terrible thought crossed her mind. Was it possible that he was angry enough to sue for breach of promise?

'And I did not just want a wife—there was more to it than that.'

'How? What else did you want?'

'A union with a respectable, dynastic family name. You've heard the nickname,' Santos added when she looked at him askance, a frown of doubt creasing the space between her brows.

'El brigante?'

A curt nod of his dark head acknowledged that she was right. 'It is not used as a compliment.'

'And that matters to you?'

She couldn't believe it. He seemed so indomitable, so unconcerned by anyone else's opinion.

'I don't give a damn,' he confirmed her suspicions. 'But I do not want my children to have to fight for their place in society as I have done. With your sister as their mother—with her family name linked to theirs—even the most conservative, most prejudiced types would have had to accept them.'

There was a bitterness in his tone that made his words ring with a harsh truth. There was no need for him to explain the prejudice he had had to live with. It was there in his voice, in the darkness of his eyes; so sharp and savage that she winced inside to hear it and the thought of what was behind it.

'I can only apologise.'

Her voice trailed away as Santos lifted broad shoulders in a shrug that expressed total indifference without any need of words. But the indifferent gesture didn't match with the dark ice in his eyes, the freezing glare that seemed to burn right through to the bone.

'You think an apology will suffice?'

'I think it would at least be—polite.'

'Ah yes, and the English, they are always so very polite. That of course makes everything right.'

'I never said that!' Alexa protested, flinching away from his black cynicism. 'But would it have been any better if Natalie had told you herself?'

'Is that what you would have done, hmm?' Santos questioned with a deadly softness that made Alexa shiver involuntarily as she caught the venom that threaded through it. 'Would you have come to me yourself? Would you have told me the truth, I wonder? Or would you have done what your sister has done and fled the country rather than face me?'

Right now, she could quite understand why Natalie had behaved as she had, Alexa told herself. Just at this moment she could imagine that she would do anything, go anywhere rather than face him. He didn't raise his voice or put any force into his words. He didn't need to. The barely reined-in anger was there in the bite of his words, contrasting with the unbelievable gentleness of his delivery. A gentleness that was somehow so much more forceful than if he had shouted.

'Natalie did what she had to do,' she managed, fighting to keep the tension she was feeling from showing in her voice. If Santos spotted any sign of weakness in her then he would be quick to take advantage of it, and she was determined to give him as little opportunity to do so as she could.

'She did what she had to do,' he echoed derisively. 'And left you to face the consequences while she ran away to be with her lover. And yet still you defend her. Still you fight her corner.'

'She's my sister.'

'Only your half-sister.'

'But family—and you know how important that is.'

'On the contrary…'

Alexa would have sworn that it was impossible for Santos's tone to become any colder, but she could practically see the ice forming on the words as he spoke them, feel the chill of his tone sear across her exposed skin.

'I'm afraid I do not share your belief in the importance of family. It is a concept that I consider to be highly overrated.'

'Another one! First love and now the family. You really are a cold-hearted bastard, aren't you?'

Just for a moment something flickered deep in his eyes. Then another blink of those heavy, hooded lids and it was gone. But it had been flashing, savage, dangerous. A look that warned her she had stepped too far over some invisible line that she wasn't aware of him having drawn on the ground between them.

Belatedly, she realised that she hadn't seen anyone who might have been his family on his side of the church. Had she blundered badly, stepping heavily on his toes, or was there something about his family that she had just not known? Something that gave a reason why they would not turn up at Santos's wedding. Her father had told her little about this man he had gone into business with, other than that he was a self-made billionaire, wealthy beyond anyone's imagining. And he had made that wealth by taking no prisoners.

'I am indeed a bastard,' he drawled silkily. 'As I am sure you are only too aware.'

'No—I...'

Oh, dear heaven, she'd made a mess of things there. Did he really believe, as his tone implied, that she might have encouraged Natalie to back out because he was illegitimate?

'And as to a family, then that was what I believed I was getting with your sister—a future family.'

Alexa hadn't been aware of having moved, but somehow her back was right up against the wall, both physically and mentally. Hastily she tried to recover lost ground.

'Look—Nat only did what I told her to.'

If his eyes had been cold before, they were pure ice now.

'You told her to run out on the marriage? What gave you the right to interfere?'

'She didn't love you!'

'Ah, yes, love—that word that seems so incredibly important to you.'

'It's more than a word,' Alexa protested. 'It's vital to life. Look, Natalie and I may only share a father, but she's still my baby sister. I was just five when she was born and she was not quite a day old when my dad put her into my arms.'

She'd fallen in love with Natalie right then and there and had vowed that if ever her sister needed anything she would be there. That she would protect her, keep her safe from harm. She'd kept to that vow for nearly twenty-one years.

'I couldn't let you make her unhappy!'

Thoughts of family gave her conscience a much needed nudge.

'I really should go and find my father—find out how Petra is doing. Do you know where they are?'

'You won't find them. They left half an hour ago.'

'They left? Then things have cleared outside? The paparazzi have gone…?'

The hopeful question faded as Santos shook his head emphatically.

'I sent them home in a car. Security will have got them through the crowd outside, but no, the Press pack has not gone.'

'If they've not gone, then why expose my father and Petra to their demands? You sent them out to face that mob…'

'I didn't want them here.'

Santos's total indifference was truly shocking.

'The Press won't be interested in your parents any more. They know now that the wedding never took place and so they guess that the real story is in here, not with them.'

Suddenly, to her complete shock and disbelief, he turned on that devastating smile, the one that left her weak at the knees, and made her heart thud unevenly.

'It's you they'll want to know about now.'

'Me? Why would they want to know anything about me?'

'They know that you went into the church instead of Natalie. They also saw you come out again with me. They'll want to know why the marriage never took place. And just what part you played in all of it.'

CHAPTER FOUR

'ME?'

He couldn't really mean that—could he?

She had thought she knew exactly why Santos had determined on holding the reception in spite of the fact that there had been no marriage to celebrate. Ruthless pride had kept him holding his head high, refusing to admit that anything had gone wrong at all. The man who didn't give a damn that he was nicknamed the brigand was also determined that no one should think he gave a damn about what had happened today.

He had told her straight out that his planned marriage to Natalie had been nothing but a marriage of convenience but he would still show the world how little he cared for his bride's defection by carrying on with the party without her. But surely it must be every bit as much of an endurance test for him as it was for her, with everyone's eyes on them, every move he made being observed and commented on.

Her disbelieving question was dismissed by another of those disarming smiles that lit his face so vividly, yet somehow managed not to reach his eyes, which remained as coldly distant and assessing as in the first moment she had met him. But even as her mind shivered in the glare of that ice-clear gaze, other, more vulnerable, more instinctual, more female parts of her were responding mindlessly to the power of that smile.

Just a curve of the lips, nothing more, and yet it warmed her deep inside, had her heart beating quicker, heat spreading right through her, melting, softening, pulsing downwards. Never before had her rational self and the unthinking, instinctive part of her been so much at war, so totally distant and on opposite sides of the fence. She knew that her sensible self should be the stronger, winning any argument without a problem, but right now it was the irrational, totally emotional—totally sensual—side that was winning..

She could tell herself that she was just imagining things. That no man could have such an instant and potent effect on her in such a short space of time. She could say it over and over again, trying to drill it into her stupid head, but even when she thought she'd succeeded, then the aching gap that yearned after Santos refused to be erased, hungering after one more glance from those brilliant eyes, the sound of his gorgeously accented voice, another of those devastating smiles.

'I thought we agreed not to waste the reception that had already been prepared.'

'We didn't agree on anything—you decreed it would be that way.'

'So if I asked you to dance, you would say no?'

'Dance?'

Was the man crazy? Did he really plan on *dancing* at this wake for his wedding?

As if on cue, the sound of music started up in the next room and as she blinked in confusion Santos held his hand out to her, palm upwards, ready to take hers.

'I hired musicians too,' he said with a faint twist to his beautiful mouth. 'I don't plan on wasting them, either. Dance with me, Alexa.'

'I—can't…'

'Can't?' His tone made it plain that he found her response impossible to understand. 'Or won't?'

The hand he had held out still hung between them, strong fingers splayed, the width of his palm tempting her to put her hand into it and feel the heat of his skin, the strength of his muscle underneath her own fingertips. Her hand twitched at her side, fighting against the sensual need to do just that and, hidden by the fall of her dress, her fingers clenched into a tight fist until her nails dug into her palm, the closest she could come to a much needed pinch to reassert reality, tell herself that she was not dreaming. This really was happening.

The day had been so totally different from the way she had expected it to go from the moment that she had got up that morning that she could almost believe she had done something like Alice and stepped through the looking glass into a new and completely unexpected world, where everything was back to front and upside down and she couldn't begin to find her way through anything or try to understand it.

'I shouldn't!'

'And why not?'

His voice had sharpened on the question, putting a sting into it that made her wince.

'You're supposed to start the dancing with your bride— your wife!'

'But my bride is thousands of miles away. Tell me something…'

His tone had changed abruptly as he took a couple of sharp, swift steps towards her, letting his hand fall back down again until it rested on the fine leather belt that encircled his narrow waist. And it was only when she saw it drop that Alexa could acknowledge the sting of disappointment that his movement brought, the way that she had really wanted to take his hand, feel its warm strength curl around her.

'If this were not my wedding day—if we had met some

other day, some other time and I had asked you to dance—would you say yes? If this was a party at which we had just met, would you dance with me then?'

Of course I would.

The words flew into Alexa's mind so fast and so clearly that she actually felt she might have spoken them aloud, or at least that they had sounded in the air so that Santos could hear them. Hastily she closed her eyes, fearful that he might be able to read her thoughts in her eyes and so know how hard and how fast she had fallen under his seductive spell.

'Would you?'

He was so close now that he only needed to murmur the question for her to hear it, and his breath stirred the wayward strands of her hair at her ear and temple as he bent his proud head towards hers. The scent of his body tormented her senses, making her think of the hard reality of the flesh and muscle concealed underneath the elegant, tailored clothing.

'Alexa, tell me…'

'Yes—yes, I would.'

'Then come…'

Once more that hand was under her nose but this time it was making an autocratic gesture, not enticing her to give way.

'Why fight?' he continued when still she hesitated. 'There is no need.'

Why fight? Alexa was asking herself the same question. The problem was that she didn't really know who she was fighting. Santos? Or herself?

She had little doubt that this was just a passing thing. That Santos was merely looking for a distraction. Something to divert his mind from the fact that he had been jilted at the altar. Even if he was truly as indifferent to things as he claimed, the public rejection had to sting his male pride if nothing else. And so he wanted something to take his mind off it. Someone to take his mind off it.

And she happened to be the nearest person.

But if she was honest then she didn't care if that was all it was, if it meant that she could have this evening. And that she could be with Santos for tonight.

'All right,' she said slowly, still not quite believing what was happening. Not at all sure where this would lead. Only knowing that she would always regret it if she turned Santos down right now. 'All right—let's dance.'

When Santos took her hand in his and she felt the warmth and strength of his fingers close around hers, the little excited judder that her heart gave in her breast told her that she had made the right decision. The decision that put a fizz of exhilaration into her veins and made her breath catch in anticipation of what was to come.

Even if at the end of the day when the clock struck midnight her coach would turn back into a pumpkin, her clothes into rags and she would have to run back home, tonight Cinderella would go to the ball. Tonight she would dance with the prince and if at midnight it all came to an end and proved to be the fantasy she deep down knew that it was then at least she would have had tonight.

'Let's dance,' Santos agreed and a rich note of satisfaction ran through the words, deepening his exotic accent and turning the words into a tiger's purr of pleasure. One that made her blood run thick with sensual reaction.

She even forgot about the way that her feet ached, the way the straps of her shoes dug into her skin as she walked beside him through the wide, marble-floored hall, heading towards the sound of the music.

But as they passed the big wooden doors leading outside, she saw how they were flung open and at the bottom of the short flight of steps a big, sleek limousine was drawn up, engine idling, waiting for some guest who was leaving early.

Seeing it, she slowed her footsteps, her mood altering

subtly. Outside the darkness was gathering, the growing shadows of the evening reminding her that this strange, unbelievable day, in which nothing had gone the way she had expected it, was starting to come to a close. And she couldn't forget that somewhere out there, in the sanctuary of their hotel room, her father and Petra would be feeling the aftermath of the day's events just as she had been doing.

And, charming or not, Santos was still the ruthless creature who had earned his notorious nickname. The man whose connections with her father had turned Stanley Montague into a shadow of the man he had once been.

'Alexandra?'

Santos had sensed her change of mood, the way that her steps were dragging. He paused and looked over his shoulder at her, not turning, his powerful body still positioned in a way that declared his intention of moving on just as soon as he could.

'Perhaps I should go back.'

'No.'

'But I should find out how my dad is…'

'No!'

It was far more emphatic this time, for all that he hadn't raised his voice above a conversational tone.

'You will not leave.'

'But Santos, I really think I should. So if you could just arrange for a car to be…'

She broke off in shock as she saw the fierce shake of his dark head, the obdurate set to the beautiful mouth, all trace of softness driven from it by the way it was clamped tight, the tautness of every muscle in his jaw.

'There will be no car.'

'Oh but surely you have more than one…' Alexa began to protest, the word dying on a gasp of shock as she realised what he had said.

Not there isn't another car. But *there will be no car.* He

wasn't just saying that it would be difficult to provide transport for her but that he wasn't prepared to.

'What do you mean, no car?'

Digging in her heels both mentally and physically, she refused to move, trying to tug her hand free when it seemed that he would march on, taking her with him. But although Santos too slowed to a halt, his grip on her hand tightened so that she couldn't free herself. 'You can't keep me here!'

'I thought that you wanted to stay.'

His voice was soft but there was a hint of steel threaded through it, and something in his eyes sent a warning that made her shiver. Did she want to stay? A moment ago she had been so sure. Now she was forced to wonder...

'I think perhaps—'

'I think perhaps not,' Santos cut in, not letting her complete the sentence. 'They didn't ask you to go with them. So you have no need to leave—not until I say so.'

But that was just too much, and hearing the arrogant declaration, Alexa brought up her head, eyes widening as she glared her defiance into his handsome face.

'What gives you the right to say when I can come and go?'

No, he'd made a wrong move there, taken the wrong tone with her, Santos told himself. She was not going to let him get away with that. An unexpected sense of admiration tugged at his mind as he acknowledged the glare of defiance in her eyes, the way her head had gone back. If he was not careful he would lose her and he didn't want to let her get away, not until he was sure that she was his. Right now she looked like a nervous mare, one of the thoroughbreds he bred at his stud, when something had spooked her. Even her nostrils flared.

He was going to have more of a challenge with this sister than he had ever expected. And the truth was that he liked the idea of that. He anticipated the prospect of having to work to win her over. She was already so much more intriguing than her sister. The end result would be worth the effort.

'It's not that I have the right.'

The faint twitch of Santos's mouth at the corners was either amusement or an admiring acknowledgement of her boldness in defying him, Alexa couldn't decide which.

'Maybe I'm not ready to let you go.'

Which was so far from the response that she had expected that it had her gaping in stunned silence, unable to believe that she had heard him right. Had he really said…?

'What do you mean by that?'

'I told you. You're here because I want you here.'

And he always got what he wanted. But why did he want her here? What did he want from her?

'So you stay until I say you can go.'

And with a sudden movement he reached out and kicked the door closed, shutting off the way out and shutting her in with him. But even as the heavy wood slammed into place, that smile was still there, curving his lips, warming his eyes unexpectedly.

'Come, now, Alexa,' he mocked when he heard her gasp of shocked horror. 'What do you think that I am going to do to you? Ravish you right here on the floor in front of all my guests?'

The hand that held hers moved slightly, twisting until his thumb was curved into her palm, smoothing the sensitive skin with a gentle touch. A touch that sent pulses of fire prickling like an electrical current along every nerve.

'I am simply asking you to stay—to dance with me—to share the evening with me.'

I'm not ready to let you go… The words that she still couldn't quite believe that Santos had actually spoken—to her—swung round and round in her head until she felt dizzy just to think of them.

You're here because I want you here.

Oh, who was she trying to kid? She *wanted* to stay, she might as well admit it. Cinderella wanted to stay at the ball—and she wanted to spend more time with this man who, if he wasn't actually Prince Charming, was certainly the most exciting, most glamorous, most devastating male she had ever seen in her whole life.

The hollow, empty feeling that had been left behind when the fizzing excitement evaporated was now filled with a sensation like the frantic fluttering of a million butterfly wings. She was no longer as worried and fearful as she had been just moments before, but her stomach clenched in apprehension and uncertainty at the thought of the evening ahead of her.

Could she handle this? Could she cope with a man like Santos? The sort of man who was light years away from any man she had ever met before and who lived the sort of life that she had never experienced. Could she cope with even one evening in his company? But could she live with herself if she chickened out now?

Now everything was changed. And it seemed, impossibly, that Santos felt something too. But with a man like him she was in out of her depth and she knew it. Everything that was sensible in her make-up, every shred of self-preservation was screaming at her to go now, leave while she still could. But at the same time every essential and most fundamental feminine cell in her body was begging her to stay. And the resulting tension, the tug of war between them, threatened to tear her in two.

Beside her, Santos moved again, lifting her hand and letting it rest against the hard warmth of his chest, so that she could count every regular, heavy beat of his heart as he looked deep into her eyes.

'Just a dance, *belleza*. Is that too much to ask?'

And when he smiled down at her she knew she was lost and there was only one answer she could give.

'No, of course it's not too much.'

Just a dance… But would that dance mark an ending or a beginning? She only knew that she would not be able to rest until she found out.

CHAPTER FIVE

AN ENDING OR a beginning?

The reception was over, everyone had left, but she still had no idea of what the answer to her question could be.

Alexa hurried down the curving stone steps that led from the terrace to the swimming pool, anxious to get onto the lower level of the garden where she would be hidden from sight by the shadows and the darkness. She needed time on her own to snatch in deep, much needed breaths of air, cool her burning cheeks, and hopefully calm the racing pulse that was throbbing at her temples and making her heart thud against the walls of her chest.

She needed time to think. Time to collect her thoughts and try to bring them under some sort of control.

Reaching the tiled area that surrounded the pool, she settled down on one of the wooden seats and kicked off the crippling shoes, sighing deeply as her cramped toes were freed and the pressure of the straps over her feet eased. If only she could ease the confusion in her mind as easily.

She was supposed to be the sensible one—the level-headed, thoughtful, grown-up daughter of the Montague family. She had never felt this way before. Never known anything like the explosion of sensation that had blown up right in her face in the time she had known Santos Cordero.

'Time? What time?' Alexa asked herself on a shaken laugh, lifting her face to stare up at the moon that shone its cool, clear light down onto the still water of the pool. She had barely known Santos more than a day, had only been in his company for a few hours at most, and yet somehow he had rocked her world and her sense of any sort of reality.

Nothing in the few gentle relationships—she could hardly even call them romances—that she had experienced had ever knocked her off her feet like this. Nothing had prepared her for the sensation of being emotionally whirled up into the air, spun round and round and finally dropped back down to earth to find that nothing at all was the same as it had been before.

And that was why she was here, in the darkness, trying to snatch some deep, calming breaths, trying to centre herself again, trying to see if she could find the Alexa she thought she was, or discover whether that Alexa had been totally destroyed by the passionate, sensual volcano that had suddenly erupted inside her head and her heart.

And all for the worst possible man in the whole world. A man she neither trusted nor truly liked. A man who lived up to his nickname of *el brigante* in both his business life and, it seemed, his private one.

'Alexandra?'

The voice, male, beautifully accented, came from above her, from the terrace that she had just left. Of course, she knew instantly who it was. Already that tone, that accent, the true sound of his voice was etched onto her brain, impossible now to hope to erase.

'Alexa!'

She wanted to stay silent, stay hidden. She didn't feel ready to face him, particularly not now when she was alone with him, when there was no one else here; no one to dilute the powerful impact of his presence.

She'd watched the fleet of elegant cars arrive at the door

of the house, watched all the other guests get in and drive away, and all the time Santos had kept her by his side, his hand on her arm, as he said goodbye, shook hands, watched them leave. Each time a new car had appeared she had hoped that this would be her chance to escape. To leave and hurry back to the hotel, where she would be able to go to the haven of her room and sit quietly, reflecting on all that had happened.

She had to wait for a car because as a bridesmaid she hadn't brought a bag with her, no money—nothing. So she was totally dependent on whatever Santos might decide.

But never once had Santos turned to her, held the car door open, helped her into it. Instead he had seemed oblivious of her presence at his side until she had finally had enough and stepped forward, tugging on his arm.

'I hope you have a car for me soon,' she'd begun, the need to be gone making her voice rough and uneven. 'I need to get back...'

The words died on her tongue as she saw his glittering eyes flash over her in cool assessment as he shook his dark head.

'Not yet.'

'Not yet?' she could only echo in shock and consternation. 'What do you mean, not yet?'

'We have things to discuss,' he'd said.

'We do?'

That dark head moved in agreement and he reached out to touch one finger to her cheek.

'We do.'

Before she could take it any further he had turned back to another departing guest, switching on a smile that had none of the stunning impact she had seen earlier. And unless she created a scene, throwing a tantrum in front of everyone, there was nothing she could do but wait and watch everyone else leave while inside her head the words that Santos had used earlier circled round and round.

I'm not ready to let you go... You're here because I want you here.

Then she'd taken them as a compliment. Now she was no longer so sure. Had she been here all afternoon because he wanted to use her company to distract him from the public stab at his pride that had been his jilting at the altar? Or was she, as a slow, creeping sense of dread was starting to make her fear, here as some sort of prisoner, the reasons for which she couldn't begin to guess?

'What are you doing down here?'

Staying silent hadn't worked. He'd known she was here all the time. Either that, or some faint movement she hadn't been aware of making had given her away.

Just the sound of his footsteps coming swiftly down the flight of stone steps, bringing him to her side, made her whole body quiver in response.

'I needed a break—a breath of air.'

'I know how you feel. It's been a long day.'

There it was again, that note in his tone that suggested the reception that had now come to an end had been a strain for him too.

He came to sit beside her, his lean, strong body a darker, bulkier shadow in the gathering dusk, and on the still air she caught a waft of the scent of his skin, clean and warm and faintly musky. Instantly she was transported back to the moments earlier, inside his beautiful house, when she had been held in his arms as they danced. She had been so near to him then that she had felt his breath on her skin as he bent his head close to hers, and the strong, steady thud of his heart under the hard ribcage had beat under the touch of her hand so that she had sensed her own pulse rate kick up instantly in response.

She had felt surrounded by him, enclosed by his touch, lost in the sight, the sound, the feel of him. And the sensation had overwhelmed her. She didn't like the way that he made her feel, and yet at the same time it was all that she wanted to feel.

And it was a sensation that, disturbingly, was creeping over her again as Santos came close once more. Her fingers itched to reach out and touch the hard strength of his arm in the white shirt that gleamed in the moonlight. She wanted to feel the warmth of his skin, inhale its scent on each indrawn breath. She wanted to know what that beautiful mouth tasted like, how it felt to tangle her fingers in the dark fall of his hair and press their tips against the fine bones of his skull. She wanted it so much and yet at the same time it terrified her to be feeling so out of control, to have lost so much of herself.

'But those were all your friends…'

And family, she had been going to add but, recalling his reaction earlier, she swallowed down the words hastily, not knowing whether they were safe to let fall or not.

'If they were real friends, do you think I would have needed to go through the farce of holding a reception for a wedding that hadn't taken place? Too many of them were business acquaintances, people it is important for me to know.'

'That's a very cynical approach.'

'I'm a very cynical man.'

The harshness of his tone made her catch her breath against the impulse to ask just what had made him that way. What had turned him into a man who saw marriage as a business arrangement, the way to provide himself with an heir without any need for or thought of love? But every instinct warned that he wouldn't welcome the question from her, and right now she didn't want to risk pushing him too far when she didn't know what his mood might be. Better to be careful when she felt as if she was treading on eggshells.

'Someone once told me that to become cynical you first had to be an idealist and it was the loss of those ideals that created the disillusionment.'

'Truly?'

Santos's harsh bark of laughter made her flinch inside.

'Then I fear I must be the exception that proves the rule. I was born without any ideals to lose. And if I'd had them, they would not have lasted very long as I grew up.'

'That sounds a very sad way to live.'

'While you were born with stars in your eyes and a belief in fairy tales and a happy-ever-after?'

She had very nearly convinced him, Santos reflected disbelievingly. She had caught him off guard and actually sounded as if she had meant what she had been saying. It must be the effect of the moonlight or the glass of two of wine he'd drunk. He wasn't usually so easily conned.

'No fairy tales.' Alexa shook her head. 'I'd be a fool to think that, wouldn't I, with my mum and dad's example before me?'

Claro—he'd forgotten that she was the daughter of Montague's first wife. The marriage that had ended in divorce.

'What happened?'

'Petra happened.' Her tone was wry. 'From the minute she came into Dad's life he couldn't think straight. He tumbled into an affair—and when he found out that Petra was expecting Nat, he came straight home and told my mother that he wanted a divorce.'

'And how did that make you feel?'

'How do you think it made me feel? You have to understand, I was four—I'd lost my daddy. He'd walked out on us to live with someone else.'

Oh, he understood all right. So much more than she could imagine.

'You didn't want to be with him—live in London?'

The look she turned on him was pure bemusement.

'I wouldn't have it given.'

When she saw his faint frown of confusion, her mouth curved into a quick smile.

'It was the last thing I wanted,' she explained. 'That was the way Petra wanted to live but it wouldn't have suited me. Besides, Petra wouldn't have wanted me and I wanted to stay with my mother. She needed me.'

'She took it badly?'

'That's an understatement! Dad broke her heart and for a long time she almost gave up on things.'

'And yet you still believe in love?'

This time her smile was wider, the light in her eyes brighter, making them a glowing, soft green.

'It didn't stay that way. Mum did eventually meet someone else. They've been married ten years now, and I've never seen her happier. And even if Petra isn't exactly my sort of person…' Her tone made it plain that this was a careful understatement. 'Dad adores her and he's never looked at any other woman since. Mum and Dad married the wrong people first time round. So, yes, I'd like to think that there's someone for us all out there.'

'And is there someone for you?'

'Me?'

She looked flustered by the question, turning wide, surprised eyes on his face. And suddenly he knew a momentary sense of unease at the thought that there might be some man she was seeing. Not that he doubted that he could make her forget about any rival if there was one. It would just be an unwanted obstacle that he would have to get rid of.

'No—there's no one.'

Her gaze dropped, eyelids half closing as she answered, and he was glad that she didn't catch the faint smile of satisfaction that he couldn't quite suppress. At least Natalie had spoken the truth when she'd said that her sister was unattached. But the suddenly down-bent head brought the unfortunate and unflattering hairstyle yet again to his attention, making him frown in disapproval.

'Come here…' he said softly, that sense of satisfaction growing as he saw the way her head came up sharply, her eyes locking with his in surprise.

Deliberately he held that shocked gaze for a moment longer, wondering if she knew that her thoughts were so transparent, able to be read only too clearly in her eyes. She thought he was going to kiss her; it was written all over her face. She thought he was going to kiss her and if he did then she wouldn't object. In fact, she *wanted* him to kiss her, so much so that those soft, rose-tinted lips had actually parted in anticipation. He could kiss her now and she wouldn't do a thing to stop him. On the contrary, she would actively encourage him.

Which was precisely why he was not going to do it. Oh, he wanted to kiss her. It was quite surprising—almost shocking—how much he wanted to kiss her. But he wasn't going to give in to that desire. She was interested now, willing even, but he wanted her more than interested, more than willing. He wanted her eager, and keen—he wanted her hungry and needing. He wanted her totally hooked so that when he made his move he could reel her in without her even having realised that she had been caught.

This sister was not going to escape him. This one was not going to run out on the deal before they even got to the altar.

'This has to go…'

Reaching out, he buried his fingers in her hair, found one of the pins—many pins, to judge by the way that the ornate style had been ruthlessly held in place throughout the afternoon and the evening, with just a few soft brown tendrils escaping from the enforced confinement. With care he eased it from its place then tossed it aside into the grass that edged the tiled pool surround, and started hunting for the next one. Although he carefully kept his attention apparently fixed on the task in hand, he was well aware of the way that her expression had changed, her face dropping, that anticipatory light leaving her eyes and something very close to disappointment clouding them.

Which was just what he wanted.

Another pin found and tossed aside. And another.

And with each one that loosened he could bury his fingers deeper in the smooth strands. Her hair really was amazingly silky; it slid underneath his fingertips like slippery satin, fine and sleek and so sensual to the touch. And as the strands were released, falling loosely around her face, down onto her shoulders, they gave up a soft, clean perfume, a mixture of some tangy citrus and an intensely feminine scent, one that immediately gave him a kick of sensuality as he recalled that it was the way her skin had smelt up close as he had held her in his arms when they danced. The twisting feeling low down in his body was so unexpected, so powerful that for a moment he paused, fingers still tangled in her hair as he fought down the very primitive masculine response.

'I'm surprised you don't have a blinding headache after keeping your hair pinned up like this all day.'

He made himself say it calmly, his tone under control; he even let himself stroke his fingers along the silky strands, enjoying the feel of it against his skin, making her perfume rise to his nostrils again.

'I have—had,' Alexa admitted. 'I've been wanting to pull the pins out all afternoon.'

Instinctively she arched her neck, pressing her skull back against his fingers and shaking her head to feel the freedom of the now loose hair.

'That feels so much better.'

Santos fought a battle with himself against the urge to tangle his fingers in the tumbling mane, twisting it to hold her just where he wanted her while he kissed her newly softened mouth. But he did allow himself to comb his hand through it, adding to the tousled effect that fell around her face. The

looser hairstyle, the touch of disarray suited her far more than
the way it had been tightly drawn back from her face.

'Then why did you ever wear it like that?'

'Oh, it was Petra's idea. She planned everything for this
wedding. She wanted it to be perfect for…'

Her voice faded away and he saw the hesitation and uncertainty in her eyes as she looked up at him, white teeth
digging into the swell of her bottom lip.

'You can say her name,' he said softly. 'The world won't
come to an end if you mention your sister. So everything had
to be perfect for a wedding Natalie wasn't going to attend.'

'No…'

That made her bite into her lip even more and, unable to
stop himself, he reached out a finger and laid it across her
mouth, easing it away from the sharp teeth that worried at it.

'Don't,' he said, as much to himself as to her, because no
sooner had he touched the softness of her skin than he wanted
to linger, to stroke his fingertip along her mouth, feel its soft
flesh give underneath his touch, perhaps even slide into the
moist warmth at one corner. That way she would be forced to
taste him, to know the flavour of his skin against her tongue.

The need to taste her too, to know the softness and the
warmth of her mouth under his, was like a savage clutch on
his senses, tugging them into burning life. He wanted to take
that slightly trembling mouth and crush it underneath his until
it quivered in a totally different way, shaking in raw surrender
to the passion he awoke in her. But still he held back. And he
knew that that piqued and provoked her from the way that her
elegant brows drew together in a quick, faint frown, one that
she immediately hurried to smooth out again.

'I don't think she planned to run out on you when she
agreed to the wedding.'

'You don't?'

'No.'

The word snagged in her breath, making her gasp as she spoke. Her reaction was as much to what Santos was doing as to the things she was trying to say. Those wickedly enticing, tantalising hands were still in her hair, smoothing and stroking, and every inch of the surface of her skin tingled in sensual reaction to the feel of his touch.

And she had been so sure that he had been about to kiss her just a moment before. The way that that strange, light-eyed gaze had lingered on her mouth had made her throat dry in shock and anticipation. She could almost feel a sensation as if his lips were touching hers, so intent was that stare, almost a physical caress in itself.

'She wanted the wedding to start with—wanted you.'

'Until you persuaded her otherwise.'

Something had changed, altering the atmosphere dramatically. His hand had stilled as he spoke and without the slow, hypnotic stroking she suddenly felt a chill creeping over her skin. There was something she had been forgetting—that her mind had dodged away from, but she should have been thinking of it all along. A man like Santos wasn't likely to simply accept a platonic relationship. Not with the woman he had planned on marrying.

'Don't!'

In a purely instinctive reaction she pulled her head away from his caressing hand, rounding on him sharply and wincing as a few tangled strands caught on his fingers and tugged painfully at her scalp.

'Stop it!'

Shaking himself free from the clinging tendrils, Santos lifted both his hands, fingers spread wide, but the dark mockery that gleamed in his eyes in the moonlight made a nonsense of the gesture of apparent surrender.

'And what precisely, *querida*, am I supposed to stop?'

It was meant to provoke and it succeeded.

'If you think that I want to be mauled by someone who was my sister's lover—or that I'm going to let into my bed any man who has only just left hers then you've got another think coming. I…'

Her voice died in painful embarrassment as she saw the look that crossed his face, narrowing his eyes and clamping his sensual mouth into a thin, hard line. Too late she realised the recklessly stupid mistake she had made, the way she had given away far more of the path down which her thoughts had been going than was safe for any sort of self-preservation or hope of retaining her composure. Biting down hard on her tongue, she could only be grateful for the way that the gathering shadows of the night and the pale light of the moon drained all the colour from the world and so, she prayed, hid the hot rush of blood into her face as she recognised just how much she had betrayed by her outburst.

'Might I suggest, *señorita*, that you wait at least until you are actually invited into my bed before rejecting any offer with the outrage of an appalled virgin?' he tossed at her with so much ice in his tone that Alexa almost felt the words like stabbing hailstones on her skin. 'For one thing, I never slept with your sister.'

'You didn't?' Embarrassment thickened her voice, heated her cheeks.

'I most definitely did not. Perhaps that was my mistake.'

'Your mistake? What sort of mistake?'

In her uncertain, apprehensive mood, Alexa found that her control of her tongue had loosened and she seemed unable to force herself to think before she spoke. Nervousness just pushed the words from her mouth before she had time to consider if they were wise, or even appropriate. Smarting from that icy put-down, she only wanted to fight back and show him that she was not the gauche, naïve girl she had let herself appear to be.

The gauche, naïve girl who had imagined him making a pass at her when in fact he had just been playing with her.

'Do you think that just because she'd shared your bed that she wouldn't be able to walk away from you? That, having had one taste of your lovemaking, she would have become so addicted that she'd have to stay around for more?'

'We'll never know, will we? And I think that you are very relieved that that is the case. I know that I am.'

'Relieved?'

Alexa frowned her horrified confusion, unable to work out just what he meant. He couldn't have seen right through to her heart and sensed the way that, in spite of herself, in spite of the fight she had against it, she had felt a flutter of something close to reassurance at the thought that her sister and Santos had never been lovers.

'You're not making any sort of sense. Why on earth would I be relieved?'

'Because, as you put it so eloquently just a moment ago, you are not going to let into your bed any man who has only just left your sister's. And now that you know that Natalie and I were never intimate, you are free to indulge your own needs, which I am sure is what you really want.'

CHAPTER SIX

No!

The rejection of his arrogant assertion was like a scream in her head, begging to be flung right in his smug, egotistical face. She had almost opened her mouth to let it out when a far too belated streak of common sense caught up with her, making her catch it back, swallow it down. Hastily adjusting her mood and dragging up some degree of control from the depths of her mind, she forced herself to look him right in the face, managing to keep herself calm in spite of the mockery that made his eyes glitter in the moonlight, the touch of a knowing smile that curved his mouth at the corners.

'I also said that I didn't want to be mauled...'

That smile grew a little wider, taking her words and her composure with it. But there was no matching lightening of his eyes, and his voice was cold and clipped when he took up the challenge in her words.

'And you and I both know that I wasn't *mauling* you. I have never mauled a woman in my life and I certainly was not doing so just now. For one thing you were enjoying it too much—'

'I was not!'

Oh, why couldn't she keep her mouth shut? She was giving herself away, digging herself in deeper with every thing she said. And he didn't believe a word of it, the sceptical expression on his handsome face, the cynically raised eyebrow said it all for him without a single thing having to be spoken.

'I was relieved to have my hair unfastened—that style felt as if it was pulling it out by the roots. And you were kind enough to help me…' she managed when he didn't speak but simply sat there, his face half in shadow, half in light, clearly waiting for her to continue. 'And—obviously it was a relief…'

'Obviously,' Santos confirmed sardonically.

And then he waited again. Waited for her to go on, to fill the silence that had descended. But there was nothing she could say, nothing that would not condemn her even further in his eyes, or make her look even more of a fool than he clearly already thought her.

'And that's it.'

'Of course it is.'

The cynical drawl made it so obvious that he didn't believe that was it at all. And seeing the way his glittering eyes swept over her, seeming to sear off a much needed protective layer of skin cells, made Alexa shift uncomfortably in her seat, a sensation like cold pins and needles prickling its way down her spine.

'Anything more is strictly in your imagination.'

The way he inclined his head in what looked like agreement but actually said exactly the opposite was positively the last straw. She couldn't sit here like this any longer, seeing the dark amusement in his eyes, listen to the taunt in his voice.

'And now I'd like to go back to the hotel.'

Pushing herself up from the bench, she got to her feet. Or, rather, she tried to get to her feet. But she had forgotten the way that her feet had been aching, the painful pressure that her shoes had put on her toes and heels, which was why she had kicked them off as soon as she had sat down. Freed from the cramped tightness of the leather, her feet had swollen and the raw spots were now fully exposed. As she tried to stand on the cool tiled surround, the force of her own weight only made things so much worse, so that she couldn't hold back a yelp of distress as pain shot through her feet and made her close her eyes in distress.

'What the…'

From behind her eyelids she sensed rather than saw the way that Santos got sharply to his feet, his hands coming out instinctively as she swayed, almost dancing on the spot to avoid putting any more pressure on the soreness of her heels and toes.

'What is wrong?'

'My feet…'

It was all that she could manage through stiff, taut lips that she had clamped tightly shut in order to hold back the weak whimper of distress at the pain. And when she opened her eyes to look up at him, seeing what looked like genuine concern in his shadowed face, the hope of saying anything more slipped right away from her in the blink of an eye.

'*Pies?*' Santos glanced down, apparently noticing for the first time the fact that she was barefoot, with her shoes tossed over to one side, almost hidden underneath the bench. 'Here— sit down again.'

Strong hands pushed her back onto the seat and she sank down with a sigh of relief as the movement took the pressure off her feet and enabled her to lift them up slightly, taking them off the ground once again.

'Let me see…'

Alexa could only blink in confusion and disbelief as in a stunningly graceful move Santos went down on one knee before her. Her heart thudded painfully in her chest as he leaned forward and picked up both feet, cradling them softly in his hands as he angled them towards the light. His touch was cool and gentle, soothing to the raw patches on her skin.

'*Madre de Dios!*' he cursed under his breath, the angry sound reaching her in the stillness of the night. 'What has happened here?'

The change of mood from the taunting of just moments before was so swift, so unexpected that it made her head come up sharply. And it was only when she saw how the outline of the moon had blurred so unexpectedly that she realised that sudden moisture was swimming in her eyes in response to the gentleness of his tone.

'My shoes...' she managed through a voice that was thick with the effort to hold back the tears. That earned her a swift, searching upward glance at her face as Santos caught the rough sound.

If he showed any sympathy, if he was kind, then it might just finish her, Alexa admitted to herself. After the mocking attack earlier, just the thought of it made her head spin.

'Your shoes!'

To her relief his tone was far from kind. He sounded coldly angry, disbelieving, appalled even. 'You wear shoes that do *this* to your feet?'

Blinking hard, Alexa peered down at the foot he was holding up for her to see. The damage was far worse than she had anticipated, she acknowledged reluctantly, wincing inwardly at the sight. Her skin was rubbed red raw, the pattern of the straps almost etched into her skin, and there were spots here and there where the pressure had actually been so great that it had taken off the surface.

'I didn't realise they were that bad.'

But Santos wasn't listening. Instead he had reached under the bench and pulled out the offending shoes, frowning down at them in dark disapproval. The straps looked impossibly delicate as they dangled from his big, tanned hands. It was hard to believe that they could have inflicted such devastation on her feet.

'What the devil possessed you to wear instruments of torture like these? You must have known they would cripple you.'

'They were fine when I tried them on. But I'm not used to heels—or all those straps.'

To be honest, she'd never thought to wear them in, and the stress of the day, the tidal wave of events that had overtaken her had made it impossible to dash back to the hotel or find some other, more comfortable footwear.

He was looking down at the shoes that he still held in his hand, the dark frown that had drawn his brows together deepening as he did so.

'You danced with me…'

'Yes, I did. But…'

Alexa couldn't see where he was going with this.

'You danced with me, wearing these damn shoes. You tore your feet to ribbons…'

'I…'

I didn't notice, she had been about to say and it would have been the truth. In those moments she had felt as if she was dancing on air and any discomfort in her feet had just not registered on her pleasure-hazed brain. But to admit that was walking right into a trap. It was just giving him more ammunition for the arrogant assumptions he had been making earlier.

'They weren't hurting then. It was only when I came out here. I think that walking across the grass, coming down the steps…'

He didn't believe her, of course; his expression said that, the look he slanted at her from those pale, gleaming eyes making the words shrivel up on her tongue.

'Come here,' he said, holding his hands out to her.

When she hesitated, unsure of what he planned, he muttered something rough and impatient under his breath. Then he stooped towards her, the bulk of his body blotting out the sight of the moon, the scent of him enclosing her, the soft fall of his hair brushing against her cheek in a way that sent a sensual shiver running down her spine. Tucked under the bench, her toes curled in uncontrollable response to his nearness.

What are you doing…? She said the words inside her head, and she tried to speak them aloud but even though she opened her mouth her voice failed her and she didn't even manage a sound. But then he bent even more, sliding his hands underneath her and lifting her bodily from the seat, taking her high into the air until he held her hard against his chest, his arms like steel bands underneath her, supporting her weight with impressive ease.

'What are you doing?'

This time she managed the words, feeling them pushed out of her by the rush of shock and confusion, the heated pounding of her pulse in response to this unexpected closeness.

'Taking you inside.'

He sounded surprised that she had even had to ask. Wasn't it obvious what he was doing? his tone implied.

'You can't walk on those feet, so this is the best way to get you indoors before you injure yourself any more.'

'But—'

'*Silencio!*' The command was hard, sharp. She would be a fool to ignore it, that was plain. 'This is what is happening—no argument.'

No argument now, maybe, Alexa thought as he carried her back up the steps towards the house, but when they got back inside she would find plenty of argument.

However, it was a struggle to collect up any rational thoughts to do so as every cell in her body seemed determined to respond to the closeness of Santos's hard male body, the strength of his arms supporting her, the wall of his chest pressed up against her cheek. Under her ear she could hear the steady, heavy thud of his heart and her own pulse seemed to set up a matching beat so that she wasn't sure where his heart rate ended or hers began. After a long and difficult day she knew a weak and foolish urge to simply lay her head against his strength, close her eyes and let everything drift. But a strong sense of self-preservation demanded that she should not give in to it. There was something here that she didn't quite understand, some thread of darkness running through everything Santos said or did. And she needed to get to the bottom of it before she could allow herself to relax—if ever.

'Here...'

The lights inside the house dazzled after the gathering darkness outside, making her blink and bury her face against his chest once more. So she felt the change in his movements but only registered slowly what it meant, realising too late that he had carried her upstairs.

'Now, wait a minute...'

Her head came up again sharply, the words snapping from her as he kicked open a door.

'Just what do you think you're doing...?'

'I'm trying to do something about your feet.' Alexa could hear the faint touch of mocking laughter in Santos's voice, setting her teeth even more on edge. 'You need to have those cuts cleaned, and—'

'In a *bedroom*?'

She tried to struggle free but had her attempts thwarted when Santos simply dumped her down onto the soft, yielding surface of a wide double bed.

'I'll need water and cloths—both in the bathroom,' he explained in a tone of such exaggerated patience that made his words anything but tolerant, 'and you might need *esparadrapos*—sticking plasters. Besides which...'

His arm swept in a wide circle to indicate the huge room and its décor.

'I can assure you that is not *my* room!'

Not unless he had suddenly developed a predilection for pink and frills, Alexa admitted, forcing herself to subside back onto the bed.

He was right in one thing, she acknowledged privately. Her poor feet did need attention. She'd been a fool to keep on wearing the shoes when they had started to rub so badly, but then she had had no real choice. Her only other shoes were miles away in the hotel where she had prepared to be bridesmaid at the wedding—such a long, long time ago, it now seemed. And unless she was to go back there barefooted then she needed something to help make her more comfortable.

So she bit her lip and kept quiet, submitting to Santos's ministrations, determined not to let him or anything he said or did get to her in any way.

And that was a resolution that she found impossible to stick to. If she thought that Santos's touch had been gentle before, then now it was soft as a caress. The warmth of the water and antiseptic ointment soothed and numbed the raw patches on her skin, and the sticking plasters he applied seemed to have magical healing properties in them.

But she would have been a liar if she hadn't admitted that she was far more affected by the sight of this dark, stunning man kneeling at her feet once again, and tending to her injuries with the gentleness of a lover. The urge to reach out and touch him, to stroke her hands across the black silk of his hair, or along the line of his jaw, was almost more than she could bear. She had to actually slide her hands underneath her thighs to keep them safe from straying into that dangerous temptation. And then when he finished, sat back on his heels, looked up into her face and directed that devastating smile straight at her, she felt her heart seem to stop for a moment, making her catch her breath in shock.

'I think that will help.'

'It will do more than help,' she managed in a voice that sounded as if it was about to break in the middle. 'They feel wonderful.'

'I'm glad.' Santos pushed himself to his feet, took the bowl from the small table on which it stood and headed for the bathroom to empty out the cooling water. 'So now we can talk.'

How had he done that? Alexa wondered. How had he

managed to inject a note into the otherwise innocuous words that made her whole body tense, every nerve stretching tight and tingling in wary apprehension, even the fine hairs on her skin lifting uneasily?

'Talk about what?'

'About where we go from here.'

Santos came to lean in the doorway, hooded silver eyes fixed on her face as she swivelled round on the bed to face him.

'The only place we go from here is downstairs…' And preferably right out of the house. 'I have no wish to be alone with you!'

'But I thought that was the plan all along, *querida.*'

The words were hissed at her with an icy control that transformed him totally. Suddenly the concerned man whose gentle touch had brought tears to her eyes had vanished and in his place was the cold-eyed, hard-faced fiend who had sent shivers down her spine in the first moment she had been introduced to him.

The man she had wondered how her sister could possibly love.

How anyone could possibly love.

And yet somehow throughout the day her opinion had changed. She had even found herself attracted to this man. Had wanted him to kiss her, to hold her.

So which one was the real Santos?

There was a nasty, slimy sensation crawling over her skin as she faced the fact that the man she had felt herself so drawn to was in fact the performance planned to deceive. And that she, like a stupid, gullible fool, had fallen straight into the trap he had set for her.

'Plan? What plan? I don't know what you're talking about. I don't know of any plan.'

'No? Forgive me if I don't believe you, *querida*, but I refuse to believe that your parents didn't have a back-up plan.'

'A back-up plan to what?'

Had the man gone mad? Was he seeing conspiracy where there was none? And if so, who exactly were the conspirators?

'They must have known that your sister was likely to run at the last minute, or perhaps that was what was meant to happen all along. And then what was I supposed to do? Take one look at the bridesmaid and fall head over heels so that I would forget about Natalie?'

'No.'

Alexa shook her head so that her loosened hair flew wildly around her face.

'No way!'

But Santos obviously wasn't listening. One more of those arrogant flicks of his hand dismissed her protest.

'So, all right,' he said coldly, 'I'll take the bait.'

'What?'

He couldn't have said what she thought she'd heard. It just wasn't possible that he meant...

'There was supposed to be a wedding, with a Montague daughter as a bride. It doesn't matter which one.'

With her hands in her lap, Alexa pinched herself hard on one palm, trying to convince herself that this was actually happening and she was not just in the middle of a bad dream. The pain was sharp, making her wince and driving away any hope that she might somehow have drifted asleep.

'You are joking!'

'No joke.' Santos shrugged off her horrified protest. 'One Montague bride is as good as any other when this was only meant to be a dynastic marriage—'

'What sort of cold-blooded monster are you?'

Alexa forced herself to stand, ignoring the agonised protests from her sore feet. She couldn't just sit there and let him tower over her with that dark look in his eyes, the curl to his lips that she couldn't tell was a smile or a sneer.

'Dynastic marriage or not—marriage of convenience or whatever—you can't just swap one bride for another because you want to!'

'Oh, but I can,' Santos assured her icily, snatching away what little was left of her breath as she struggled to inhale naturally while her heart was thudding frantically against her ribcage. 'A deal is a deal and no one breaks their word to me and gets away with it.'

But it was Natalie who had broken her promise to marry him! Alexa felt as if the world was spinning out of control and she didn't know whether she was on her head or her heels. Even if he wanted to sue for breach of promise then surely he couldn't go this far.

'Or maybe this was what you and your family had planned all along. You baited the hook with the glamorous sister, always knowing that she was going to run out on me.'

And leave him with the less glamorous, less attractive one. He didn't have to say the words—they were buried in his callous declaration, aimed at her like a slap in the face, as cold and as cruel as any physical blow.

'There was no plan. And I have no intention of marrying you.'

'You don't have any choice. It's either that or watch your family go to the wall.'

'Why aren't you listening? I don't want to marry you…'

His words made no sense and they barely registered as she flung her angry response into his arrogant, beautiful face. His look was totally blanked off, eyes opaque. And Alexa was grateful for that strange lack of expression. Anything more and she would have lost the fight she was already having not to lift her hand and lash out at him, wipe the condescension from his carved features. As it was, her fingers twitched at her sides, twisting in her skirt as she sought for control.

'I don't want anything to do with you.'

That got through to him.

'And we both know that to be a lie,' he tossed back at her, an unholy amusement lighting in those pale eyes as they gleamed down at her. 'Outside, by the pool, you were mine for the taking.'

'No, *that's* the lie! I never—'

'Oh, come, now, *querida*,' Santos mocked. 'If I'd kissed you, you wouldn't have spared a thought for your sister or for anyone else. You would have melted into my arms...'

But that was just too much. The knowledge that he hadn't seen anything other than what she had really been feeling wasn't enough to hold her back as a terrible sense of having been manipulated, played like a puppet with Santos holding the strings, blazed like a firestorm inside her head.

'A kiss maybe—but not this! This is crazy! Mad! Impossible!'

'No it is not,' Santos returned smoothly. 'To my mind it's completely possible—the perfect solution. Natalie ran out on me, but you are right here. So now you can take your sister's place.'

CHAPTER SEVEN

So NOW YOU can take your sister's place.

It was impossible. The man was mad—he had to be.

'No way! It's just not happening!'

'And why not, hmm?' Santos shot back. 'Why is that so impossible?'

'Because—because you don't know me. I don't know you.'

'I know that I like what I see and I believe that you do too.'

'Well, yes…'

The answer was snatched from her lips before she had time to consider just how foolish she was being in admitting it. The look of dark satisfaction that crossed his face, burning in his eyes, curling the corners of his sensual mouth, made her blood run both hot and cold in exactly the same moment so that she trembled as if she was in the grip of some dangerous fever.

I like what I see. Had he really said that about her? After years of living in Natalie's shadow, of hearing her sister described as the beautiful one, the one who had men buzzing round her like bees around a honey pot, it shook her rigid that a man like Santos would actually express his feelings so bluntly. But it was a huge jump from that to saying that he wanted to marry her!

'So you must see…'

'No. No, I see nothing because there is nothing to see. Nothing at all! How can there be when we have said nothing—admitted nothing—but that we like the look of—that we fancy each other? How can that mean anything? How can you claim anything so ridiculous, so preposterous, as to say that you—you've…?'

She couldn't say it, no matter how many times she opened her mouth and tried to force her tongue to form the words, she couldn't bring herself to echo the wildly impossible declaration that he had made just moments before.

Santos, however, had no such problem.

'That I'll take you as my wife? Why not? I never wanted your sister as I want you.'

'But you…' Alexa began but then the realisation of just what he had said sank into her numbed brain. 'Is that the truth?'

'Why should I lie to you, *belleza*?'

Santos's tone was suddenly soft. His gaze still held hers as he spoke, his eyes so deep and clear that she felt they were like a still, smooth pool in which she risked drowning, going in over her head completely.

Alexa wished that she could look away, but she found it impossible to drag her gaze from that mesmerising stare of his, the look that seemed to search right to the depths of her soul and know exactly what was hidden there.

'But…'

Her head was spinning, the room seeming to blur around her.

'But how can you know that? You haven't even kissed me…'

Santos pushed both hands through the gleaming darkness of his hair in a gesture that could have been taken as showing that he was relaxing, easing some of the tension that held his long body taut. But his eyes said exactly the opposite. They were as cold and sharp, as predatory as ever.

'That is something that is soon remedied.'

To her horror he crossed the room, skirting the table with a lithe, elegant movement, coming towards her with his intent clear on his face.

'No…'

Alexa's hands came up as if to ward off danger, and immediately she started backing away, taking hasty steps away from him. But the truth was that she knew that what she feared deep inside wasn't really Santos but herself. The memory of those moments in the garden was burned into her mind, and she knew she would never forget how she had felt when he leaned towards her and she had been so sure that he was going to kiss her.

If her heart had picked up a beat then, now it was thudding so hard that her blood pulsed like a thunderstorm inside her head, pounding at her temples until she was unable to think. She had wanted that kiss so much and it had stung so badly when he had withheld it at the last minute. And he had known the way she was feeling, she was positive of that.

So now he knew what he was doing as he came towards her with that look in his eye, his gaze fixed on her mouth. And she was afraid of herself, not for herself. She was afraid of her own reaction, of the way she might respond to him if he kissed her. If she felt this way already, then how much more might she feel if…when…?

So, 'No!' she said again, more urgently this time, moving backwards all the while, not looking where she was putting her feet because she did not dare to take her eyes from his face, seeing the way it was hard and set, tight with determination and resolve. 'No, Santos—I— Oh!'

The exclamation was forced from her in shock as the backs of her legs hit something—the side of the bed, from the feel of it. Knocked off balance and unable to stay upright, she suddenly plonked down onto the quilt, all the breath escaping from her lungs in a rush so that she gasped out loud as she landed.

And still Santos prowled closer, big and dark and sleekly dangerous, like some elegant hunting panther that knew it had its prey totally cornered and was enjoying delaying the moment of pouncing until the very last second.

She tried to get up, but it was as if all the bones had been removed from her legs and she couldn't find the strength to push herself to her feet. And suddenly he was there. Looming over her, with one hand each side of her, long, lean, bronzed fingers spread out over the crisp white cotton, square-tipped nails immaculate.

For the first time, seeing them this close, she noted a scar that ran across the knuckles of the right hand. Obviously made a long time before, it was just a fine, silvery line in the tanned skin, but her fingers itched to reach out and trace their way along it, and the need to ask how it had happened burned on her tongue.

But in the same moment Santos spoke her name, his voice low and soft, disturbingly cajoling, and instantly she forgot what she was thinking, every last trace wiped from her mind. The scarred hand moved, sliding under her chin, lifting her face towards his, and his dark head bent slowly, his beautiful mouth coming closer to hers inch by infinite inch.

She'd stopped breathing. Her mouth was painfully dry but her throat seemed paralysed unable to swallow, and she couldn't do anything to ease it. She was sure that even her heart had ceased to beat, though the blood still throbbed at her temples and at the vulnerable pulse point at the base of her throat. The way he held her, with his proud head, his handsome face coming between her and the light, meant that she could look nowhere but into his eyes, seeing the way that his pupils had expanded, black where they had once been silvery grey.

Suddenly afraid of what her own eyes might reveal, she lowered her lids hastily, retreating inside herself, fighting the need that simply having him so close was already sparking off inside her. But her temporary blindness only made matters so much worse, heightening every other sense to painful sharpness. She could smell his skin and the faint tang of some citrus soap or shampoo that lingered on his body, hear the soft sound of his chest rising and falling as he drew air into his lungs.

'*Belleza*,' Santos murmured and she felt his breath against her lips, snatching it in with the oxygen she needed so that she felt she could already taste him in her mouth, against her tongue.

But when his lips finally touched hers it was as if she had never known anything like it before in her life. As if she had never been kissed before, never felt the brush of a man's lips against her own at any other time, with anyone else in the world.

After the force of his approach, the power of his movements as he strode towards her, she might have expected that his kiss would be forceful too. Her whole body was tense, waiting for the impact of his mouth on hers, the feeling close to being punished for daring to challenge him, for defying his declaration that he wanted her. So it was a shock to her system when his kiss was the softest, most gentle touch she could have imagined, a butterfly-wing stroke of his lips to hers with a delicacy that tore at her heart, drawing out her soul and making her sigh her response straight into his caressing mouth..

Just one kiss and then he drew back again. And the ache of loss when he did so was almost more than she could bear, bringing an involuntary murmur of protest that there was no way she could hold back.

'Patience, *querida*...'

Never before had his voice sounded so sexy, so enticing, and behind her closed eyelids she could almost hear the smile that curved his seductive mouth.

Santos...

His name sounded in her head, never quite reaching her tongue because even as she tried to speak he kissed her again, with just the faintest increase of pressure so that her heart kicked against her ribs, her senses swimming.

Again he kissed her, and again, harder each time, until she was breathless with response and with the growing need that he had sparked off inside her. Each time his lips touched hers she wanted it to last for ever and each time he took them away again she felt as if something was breaking up inside, splintering into a thousand tiny, yearning, needy pieces.

'Santos!'

The sound of his name brought her lips against his in the first kiss she had given him and the sensation of it was like a bolt of burning lightning flashing through her, making her toes curl, her hands clench against her sides, fighting the need to reach out and touch him, to lace her hands in the midnight-dark silk of his hair, feel it curl around her fingers. Heat was building in her veins, hunger uncoiling in the pit of her stomach. And obviously Santos felt it too because he slid both hands into the fall of her hair around her face, cupping the bones of her skull and holding her head in just the right position so that he could deepen the kiss, bring her mouth open under his.

Or did she respond to him in this way? Alexa had no idea who reacted to whom and when. She only knew that now she desperately needed him to give her more than the gentle caresses that had stunned her so much at first. That she needed more than softness, than a delicacy of touch. She needed heat and hardness, strength and pressure. She needed to feel the power of his hands, the tightness of the muscles in his arms as they closed around her, lifting her from her seat.

Or did she stand up to him?

She didn't know the answer to that, only knew that somehow she was on her feet, pressed tight against the hard strength of his body, feeling the warmth of him enclose her as she drew in the clean scent of his skin.

His mouth was no longer gentle but demanding in the way she had feared it might be from the start. Now she had no fear of that demand and met it with a hunger of her own, pressure for pressure, need for need. Now her hands were free to tangle in his hair as she had wanted, but as soon as she had her wish she knew that it wasn't enough. She wanted more. Wanted to touch him everywhere, to feel the strength of muscle and bone underneath her searching fingers, slide in at the open neck of his white shirt and know the satiny warmth of his skin, the crisp feel of his body hair tickling her palm.

One of Santos's hands was in her hair, twisting to hold her still, to keep her mouth just where he wanted it, while the other roamed over her body. His tongue tangled with hers, tasting the innermost warmth of her mouth, mirroring the more intimate dance towards which they were heading. And they were heading that way. There was no doubt of that at all in Alexa's mind. This heat, this hunger, this yearning intensity could not lead to anywhere else. It was as if someone had started the countdown to a nuclear explosion and there was no way of stopping it that wouldn't result in an even more dramatic meltdown than the one they had triggered between them.

'I want you,' Santos muttered against her mouth, his accent so raw and thick that the words were almost incomprehensible.

But there was no need of words with the heated evidence of his arousal pressed against her stomach, with his hands growing harder, more demanding with every pass they made over her body. The heat of his fingers over her breast had her nipple peaking in urgent response, pushing wantonly into his palm so that the brush of his fingers was a stinging pleasure, sending sensation rushing from this most sensitive point to flood the rest of her body with need. Alexa moaned aloud at the feel of it, hearing Santos laugh deep in his throat as he caught her response against his lips, kissing it back into her mouth, his taste blending with her own until she didn't know where she ended or he began.

And that was how she wanted it in every cell in her body. The primal heat that his kisses had started within her licked along every nerve, pooling low down between her legs where a heavy, honeyed pulse of desire beat a primitive tattoo so that when he half walked, half carried her backwards to the larger settee she went with him willingly, too lost in sensation, too mindless with need to think of anything beyond the moment. And when the backs of her legs hit the side of the bed as they had done earlier she tumbled onto the downy quilt, carried further and faster with Santos's heavy weight coming down on top of her.

His hands were under her dress now, pushing the pink satin down her arms to expose her heated skin, fingertips trailing burning patterns over her body so that she writhed in unrestrained delight at the sensations his touch created.

'Want you too,' she muttered urgently, her voice not sounding like her own, it was so rough and raw with need. 'Kiss me—touch me…'

Take me, she longed to say but even now some last remaining hint of restraint kept a check on her tongue. There was no going back, she knew that deep in her soul. It would tear her apart if he stopped now, when her body was aching for him, straining towards him, almost screaming the need to know his full possession, the total union of their bodies, skin on skin, flesh against flesh, hunger matching hunger.

But she couldn't quite bring herself to voice that need. Didn't dare to put her yearning into words, to strip away the carefully protective mask she had felt the urge to wear in front of this man. Stripping her clothes off was one thing. That was what she wanted more than all the world—to be physically naked with him. But emotional nakedness was quite another matter. That was something she didn't dare reveal to him. It would be like putting her soul under a microscope and letting him dissect it with a cold, brutal steel knife.

Needy fingers fumbled with the buttons on his shirt, tugging them free with impatient movements. Exposing his skin brought a sudden rush of the warm, slightly musky scent of his skin and she inhaled it like some rich perfume, feeling the impact of it hit her as if it was a raw aphrodisiac.

'Santos…'

His tormenting hands had moved further inwards, stroking over the creamy lace of her bra, the delicate covering lasting only a second or two under his knowing fingers. Swiftly and expertly he freed the clasp at the back, easing the soft material from her swollen breasts and replacing it with the heat of his palms, cupping and lifting her in a way that no underwear could ever do. And all trace of embarrassment, all trace of thought, fled from her mind completely as he stroked caressing thumbs over each taut nipple, making her gasp aloud at the shock of stinging arousal.

She caught the faint sound of his laughter once more as he kissed her again, taking that gasp into his own mouth and swallowing it down without taking his lips from hers. And all the time his hands worked magic on her breasts, stroking, teasing, caressing until she was writhing under his touch, almost out of her mind with pleasure.

'I knew this was how it would be,' Santos muttered against her skin as that hot, demanding mouth started to move downwards, over her chin, along the sensitive line of her throat, leaving a trail of burning kisses everywhere it touched. 'Knew how it had to be.'

She felt his tongue touch her too, slick and warm, lingering over the spot where her pulse beat frantically under the delicate skin at the base of her neck. Then, shocking her into lying totally still, holding her breath in stunned excitement, he moved his caresses to the soft slopes of her breast, kisses replacing his fingers, moving slowly, sinfully, seductively upwards, until at last his lips closed over the taut bud of her nipple, drawing it into the heat of his mouth, teeth grazing it so very gently.

'Santos!'

Her use of his name was a raw, primitive sound that shocked her to hear it. She hadn't known that she was capable of being so out of control, so far from civilised, and her fingers clutched in his hair, holding him still against her. This time his laughter was a warm feathering across her sensitive nipple, making her shiver and wriggle in ecstatic response.

But she couldn't control his hands, and they were far from still, roaming even lower, stroking over the soft planes of her stomach, blunt fingertips circling her navel then dipping into the small, soft valley. She had barely caught her breath before they moved again, tracing slow, erotic patterns over her skin as they slid lower, easing the satin skirts upwards, slipping under the near-transparent panties, tangling in the dark hair that shielded the most intimate spot of her body. The spot that throbbed and burned in anticipation of the pleasure of his touch. Arching herself into those caressing fingers, Alexa sighed her contentment and encouragement, urging him onward, lower…

'Oh, yes—Santos…please…'

Eyes closed, she reached for him blindly, arms locking around his strong neck, drawing him down to her again so that his lips captured hers once more. The feel of his breath against her cheek was as hot, as raw and uneven as her own, telling her without the need for words that he was as far beyond control as she was.

'How have you done this to me?' he muttered against her mouth. 'How has it come to this so fast?'

The same questions were whirling inside her head but she didn't want to stop and consider them, didn't want to let them take root in any way that might make her pause and think, re-consider how she had come to be here. She simply wanted to feel, to experience this wild rush of passion. To know the full force of Santos's possession.

With hands that shook with need, she tugged at Santos's

clothing, wrenching the buttons of the silk waistcoat from their fastenings, pushing it aside.

His shirt followed, buttons dispensed with with more haste than finesse, the fine garment tossed aside as her hungry fingers closed over the warmth of his skin, the power of tight, clenched muscle, drawing him even closer to her.

That tormenting touch left her briefly as Santos dealt with the rest of his clothing, coming back to her before she had really realised that he had gone, the heat of his body coming over her like an enfolding wave, swamping her thought processes. She coiled around him so tightly that she could almost not tell where she ended and he began. But there was still that one, vital part of her that was hungry, empty. Longing for, needing his possession. Unable to put her need into words, she could only press herself against him, mutely imploring him to ease the agony of waiting, to take her, to take them both to the wild oblivion she could sense was just out of sight, just out of reach.

And Santos needed no extra urging. With his mouth still tight against hers, he slid one hard-muscled leg between both of hers, edging them apart to open her up to him. His arms slid underneath her pliant body, raising her slightly so that her hips cradled him, her legs curling around his.

She had barely time to snatch a breath, to gather herself, before he had thrust inwards, deep and hard, taking her high into delight, almost splintering her into ecstasy in the very first moment of their coming together.

'Santos!' His name was a cry of wonder, of shocked disbelief, as she clung to him, her heart thudding, her eyes wide, her breath shuddering in her lungs.

'Easy, *belleza*,' Santos soothed, his voice sounding as if it was fraying at the edges, coming unravelled just as she was.

And just that sound deprived her of any hope of taking anything 'easy'. Just the thought that she had had such an effect on this darkly devastating man had her moving sharply, catching his gasp of reaction in her mouth as she took him with her.

'Alexa…'

Her name was the last thing he managed as she took control from him, using the sensual power of his body, the mind-blowing impact of his kisses to take her hard and fast, driving her unerringly towards oblivion with almost terrifying concentration.

Their bodies clashed and shuddered, gasping breaths tangling together, heartbeats racing, thundering, pounding as one. Together they came to the edge and together they stayed there for one agonising moment before a single final thrust took them over, spinning them out into the whirling haze of ecstasy that seemed to turn Alexa's soul inside out and back again and again until she finally came back down to earth with a stunned and shaken sigh.

Exhausted, replete, she just wanted to lie there, to feel Santos's arms come round her again. Perhaps his kiss against her face. So the change when it came was so sudden, so shocking, so unbelievable, that it stunned her rigid, keeping her lying there with her eyes closed as Santos moved away from her. Not just to the side of the bed, not to hold her or cuddle close in any way, but up and away from her, the sound of the thud of his feet on the floor telling their own story. The cold shiver of air over her skin chilled her heated flesh, stopped her racing pulse and left her feeling lost and bereft, totally alone.

And then his stillness was so complete, so lengthy, that after a few moments his silence got through to her where she hid behind the security of her closed eyelids.

'Santos?'

It was a whisper that got as far as her lips but then she didn't dare to let it go. She was afraid to let him hear in her voice how shaken she was at what he was doing—or, rather, not doing. She didn't want him to see her shock and distress, or realise how horrified she was.

But when Santos moved at last, the faint rustle of material telling her that he had snatched up some clothing, she couldn't hold back any longer.

'What is it?'

Her eyes flew open, staring straight into Santos's cold, gleaming stare, and what she saw there chilled her right through to the bone. He had not only picked up his clothes, but had also shrugged on his shirt, pulling it closed at the front and buttoning it up with fingers that were shockingly steady and disturbingly fast. It was as if he couldn't wait to cover up, to be away from her.

'Santos—what…?'

For the space of a couple of shocked, unsteady heartbeats, he held her stunned gaze without moving, without any hint of emotion. And then his eyes dropped, surveying her exposed, half-naked body with such total disdain that she could almost feel the burn of his gaze searing off a much needed protective layer, leaving her raw and vulnerable.

'I think that will do,' he said at last, his tone as icy as his eyes.

'Do?'

Alexa couldn't believe what she was hearing, what was happening. How had the ardent, urgent lover of just moments before been suddenly transformed into this cold-eyed, hard-faced, hard-voiced stranger?

'Do in what way?'

'In every way.'

To her horror he flashed an on-off smile, barely there then gone again, into her appalled face, no trace of light reaching his eyes so that it was only a movement of his mouth with no effect anywhere else. He finished fastening his shirt, reached for his trousers and pulled them on before smoothing his palms over the shining black hair that her clutching fingers had disordered, restoring it to order. He might as well have put on a suit of armour, closing it up around his chest and throat, carefully keeping her at bay, so deliberate were his actions, distancing himself from her and practically putting up a warning sign that declared loudly, 'Go away, keep out! Trespassers will be prosecuted.' Even his stunning eyes were hidden under heavy, hooded lids, so that she could barely see them.

'I think I've made my point. In one way at least, there is someone out there for each of us. I've never known anything like that. Never.'

'And is that meant to be a compliment?'

The terrible, tearing agony of realising that it had all been just some perverted sort of test, a way of proving that she couldn't resist him—and, damn it, she hadn't been able to, had she?—made her voice shrill with self-disgust.

'Am I supposed to be grateful?'

'Not grateful, no. But you might consider it a relief because it shows that in this way at least, our marriage is not going to be the ordeal you seemed to think. In fact, you might actually enjoy it.'

'Why, you—'

She would have lost her grip on her control, would have launched herself at him in a fury, but at that moment a loud buzzing sound had Santos pulling his mobile phone from the pocket of his trousers.

'Si... Momento...'

Shockingly matter-of-fact, he turned back to Alexa.

'Perdone...I have to take this call. Wait here—I will be back in a moment and we will talk about this further.'

They wouldn't talk about it at all, Alexa told herself. And if he thought that she was going to stay here quietly and wait for him after that horrific humiliation, then hell would freeze over before she would do any such thing. But, deciding that discretion was very definitely the better part of valour and she would do best not to arouse his suspicions, she forced herself to nod briefly, avoiding the searching gaze of his eyes as she did so.

She even managed to lie still, exactly where she was, as he walked away, her heart thudding, breath catching as she prayed that he would just keep moving and that he wouldn't look around, that nothing in her edgy position, the way she was poised in readiness for flight, would communicate itself to him.

As soon as Santos disappeared through a door at the far end of the room she jumped off the bed, pulling down her dress and adjusting it, tugging her clothing back into place as she went. Looking in the mirror was the last thing that she wanted to do but practicality forced her to do just that. She could hardly walk out of here looking as if…

Oh, *hell*—looking as if she had just been indulging in the most wanton, erotic sex of her life.

She might have been doing just that, but her tangled hair, swollen lips and panda eyes were too much of a giveaway for appearing in public. She was forced to waste a few precious moments on essential repairs, all the time scarcely daring to breathe for fear that the door would reopen and Santos would come back into the room.

But at last she was on her way, running silently down the stairs, trying to work out just how she was going to get a car to take her back to her hotel.

In the end it was stunningly easy. She braved it out, speaking to the first member of staff she saw.

'Señor Cordero wants the car brought round to the front door.'

Obviously the power of Santos's name was absolute because the woman simply nodded and disappeared in a rush. There was a brief, anxious wait, a panic that perhaps he might finish that phone call and catch her. But then suddenly the sleek black limousine was there by the steps, the uniformed chauffeur getting out to open the passenger door for her, and she scrambled hastily and rather inelegantly inside, huddling down on the seat in case Santos should reappear and look around for her.

It was only as the car pulled away and headed down the drive that she allowed herself to draw in a long, shaken breath in the hope of slowing the whirling spin of her mind and look around. She couldn't quite relax until they had reached the main road and turned in the direction of Seville, and that was when she realised that she still had nothing on her feet.

The elegant and ruinously expensive shoes that had crippled her feet so painfully were still lying under the wooden bench near to the swimming pool where she had kicked them off when she had first gone outside. She had left them there when Santos had carried her inside and she had no intention at all of going back for them, no matter how much they had cost. Apart from the fact that they would tear her feet to ribbons, they now had memories attached to them that she didn't want to have to recall.

So she was sitting in the car like some sort of Cinderella on her way home from the ball, having left her shoes back there. But they weren't glass slippers, and it wasn't Prince Charming she had left behind. Instead of her coach turning back into a pumpkin it was Santos himself who had changed from seeming to be something close to the prince into the Big Bad Wolf.

All the magic she had felt earlier in the evening had evaporated, leaving a bitter taste in her mouth as the tiny dreams she had allowed herself to feel just for a moment shrivelled into ashes. And she could only pray that the wolf prince wouldn't come after her as he had hunted down Cinderella in the original fairy tale.

CHAPTER EIGHT

CINDERELLA WAS WELL and truly back from the ball.

Alexa's smile was wry as she unlocked her front door and let herself back into her cottage after a long day at work. The contrast between the luxury and style of Santos's beautiful house outside Seville and this tiny home, with its slightly shabby décor and worn appearance, couldn't have been much greater. But at least this was a home and not a showplace as the Seville house had been. A showplace with no heart, and no real warmth of any sort.

Much like its owner.

She certainly wouldn't trade one for the other any day. Not even when her own little cottage felt as chilled and unwelcoming as it did now. The central-heating timer must be on the blink again.

The weather too was as different as it could be from the mild temperatures she had left behind in Spain. Here in Yorkshire, the wind was a biting, bitter chill, and the forecast was for it to get even colder over the weekend. There were even suggestions of a storm. Certainly the sky had looked heavy enough as she had driven back up the steep winding road that led from the library to her home. She just prayed that the heating would work once she checked on it and switched it on manually.

The house was just beginning to lose the chilly edge from the temperature and she had started to prepare an evening meal when there was an unexpected ring at the doorbell.

Who could that be? She wasn't expecting anyone and the cottage was far enough from the village to deter casual callers, with no one living near enough to be described as a neighbour. Wiping her flour-covered fingers on a handy tea towel, she hurried down the corridor to answer the summons.

With no glass pane in the door to give her any clue, no way of seeing just what sort of a figure might be at the door, she had no warning. And so the sight that met her eyes when she pulled it open had her losing all her breath in one shocked gasp and taking a couple of stunned, shaky steps backwards.

Santos Cordero stood there, big and dark and large as life. Or perhaps even larger than life, because that was how he seemed with his powerful frame filling the small doorway, his broad shoulders almost blocking out the view of her slightly unkempt garden, his black hair blown wildly over his forehead by the whirling winds that howled amongst the trees. His eyes were almost as cold and bleak as the darkening sky and it seemed that the weather prediction of hailstorms had been an accurate one, with white pellets spinning in the air, and some of them had settled on his head, glistening among the black strands like melting diamonds.

'Santos!'

'*Buenas tardes, señorita.*'

If the faint flicker of something across his sensual mouth was supposed to have been an attempt at a smile then it failed completely, switching on and then off again with a speed that made her wonder if it had ever been there. His dour frown and hooded eyes seemed much more his natural expression, destroying the memory of the devastating smile she had experienced so very briefly only the week before.

But nothing could wipe away the sheer impact of the man.

Even now, huddled into a navy-blue coat, shoulders hunched against the icy winds, he was still the most shockingly handsome man she had ever seen. And his naturally golden skin seemed even more exotic when contrasted with the dull tones of the wintry landscape surrounding him.

'What are you doing here?'

She knew she sounded ungracious but shock had pushed the words from her mouth. He was the last person she had expected or wanted turning up on her doorstep. Or at least that was what her rational mind allowed her to admit to. The real truth was that some wickedly unwanted, instinctive inner response had made her heart clench in instant reaction in the moment that she had recognised his dark, stunning features.

'I came to return your property.'

Santos lifted one hand to display a silvery plastic carrier bag that looked strangely out of place in his strong masculine grip.

'My…? What property?'

'Your shoes.'

'You have to be joking! If you think that I would believe that anyone would travel all the way from Seville, fly across the Channel and then drive here, just to return a pair of shoes, then…'

She broke off hastily, choking to a halt as Santos lifted the carrier bag even higher and opened it at the top, just enough for her to be able to get a glimpse of its contents. The sight of the pale pink leather sent a hot tide of blood rushing into her cheeks. And the gleam of something darkly wicked deep in those unusual eyes only added to her embarrassment.

'You did that! There was no need!'

Santos shrugged off her protest.

'I wanted to return your property, but that was not the only reason I came here.'

'Putting them in a parcel and posting them off would have been enough.'

Belatedly, Alexa realised that she had talked across Santos, her voice covering the second part of his statement. But now the truth of what he had actually said hit home.

'It wasn't? So why else are you here?'

'Perhaps if you would let me in, then we could talk?'

The suggestion was an obvious one. Or at least it would have been if her relationship with this man was a normal one. Relationship? She didn't have a relationship of any sort with him. But politeness cost nothing and she couldn't keep him standing on the doorstep for ever in this weather. Much as she might want to.

But to invite him in suddenly seemed to have so much more significance than it deserved. Simply because he was Santos and because of the way they had parted after the reception.

'What do we need to talk about?'

'It would be easier if you let me in.'

And if she didn't let him in then he was saying nothing, that much was obvious. With a resigned sigh, Alexa held open the door.

'Come in, then…'

She had been outmanoeuvred and she knew it—and so did he. She fully expected him to murmur 'Checkmate', or whatever the Spanish equivalent was, as he moved past her into the narrow hallway.

She'd regretted her action as soon as she had opened the door. He was the last person she wanted inside her home. And yet her heart gave a strong kick of excitement as he moved past her into the confined space of the tiny hall. How was it possible to wish that he was anywhere but here in the same breath as she acknowledged the fact that now he *was* here she couldn't take her eyes off him?

The cottage had low ceilings which made him look impossibly tall, and the width of his shoulders was emphasised by the heavy jacket he wore. He brought in a rush of cold, damp air with him and as he turned to face her, she saw that wide, devastating smile on his face.

'What?' she asked sharply, that smile setting her pulse pounding, her legs feeling like cotton wool underneath her as she fought against the temptation to lean back against the wall for support. 'What's so funny?'

'Not funny, but…'

Santos leaned forward and brushed the pad of his thumb across her cheek, his touch warm and soft. And suddenly her heart seemed to stop beating, her breath coiling tight in her throat.

'You have flour on your face. There…'

He held up his hand to show her the streaks of white but apart from one brief glance Alexa couldn't look at it and away from his face. Her eyes were drawn to his, her gaze held transfixed, and although that smile had faded there was still some lingering warmth that heated her skin more than the old-fashioned central heating clanking its way through the radiators.

Memories surfaced. Memories of a beautiful Moorish-style house, a pink bedroom, and the softness of that touch that had soon become so much more. Memories she didn't want to recall and that she had to crush down with an almost vicious effort as heat flooded her face.

'Thanks…' It was a growl of embarrassment.

Automatically she raised her own hand to wipe at the spot, but then, seeing the flour on her fingers, shook her head and dropped it down again.

'Come in.' She made her tone unnecessarily brisk to hide the confusion that had her in its grip.

Santos's next move was perfectly natural, perfectly logical, but as she moved to push open the door into her sitting room he pushed the front one closed, so that it slammed into the frame with a worryingly ominous thud that made all the hairs on the back of her neck lift in sudden apprehension.

Had she made a foolish move inviting him in like this? Never before had she been so aware of the fact that the cottage was isolated and with the weather closing in around them she was very much alone. The sooner she got this over with and sent Santos on his way, the better. She was not going to offer him a drink, she resolved as she led the way into the sitting room. That would make it look as if she wanted him here.

'So what is this about?'

Alexa moved carefully to position the coffee table between herself and the big, dark man standing before her, making the sitting room look almost like something out of a doll's house with all the furniture out of proportion and far too small in contrast to his size.

'And don't expect me to believe that it has anything to do with the shoes that you used as an excuse to worm your way into here.'

'Not worm my way, *querida*.' Santos had the nerve to make his words sound like a reproach as he shook his dark head in rejection of her accusation. 'I simply said that we needed to talk.'

'But to talk about what—just why are you here?'

'Why? I would have thought that was obvious.'

Why *was* he here? Santos had asked himself that question a hundred times on the journey from Spain. He knew what had sparked the decision to make the journey. It had been made in the black fury that had descended on his brain when he had got back to the bedroom after taking the phone call. A too long, impatient phone call in which he had cut off one of his managers with harsh ruthlessness in order to hurry back to where Alexa was.

Or, rather, where he had thought Alexa was.

Instead the room had been empty, the door wide open, and no sign of the woman who had been in his arms, responding so passionately to his kisses, his caresses, such a short time before. The only evidence that she had ever been there was the dishevelled quilt, the dent in the pillow where her head had lain.

He'd known then what had happened, though he hadn't quite been able to believe it. And the red mist that came up before his eyes threatened his ability to think straight enough to believe, or to doubt. A hurried search, an even more hurried questioning of some members of staff had only confirmed his furious suspicions and that was when all rational thought had fled his brain, driven out by the roar of pure fury that totally consumed him.

She had run out on him.

A second Montague daughter had turned tail and run just like her sister. The whole family had slashed at his pride and his reputation—and taken the money he had been foolish enough to let them have at the start. Someone would have to pay.

And that someone was going to be Alexa Montague.

He could of course have simply called in her father's debts, and sent the lying fool to prison for embezzlement, as he had originally planned, but that thought no longer satisfied him. The one thing that had been clear in his mind was that he was going to find Alexa Montague.

It had been a simple matter to track down her address. Her witch of a stepmother had been only too keen to supply it, and her weak, greedy father had gone along with it, seeing his own hope of escape by doing so. Her family had handed her to him on a plate.

And as soon as she had opened the door to him this evening he had known exactly why. He had never been able to get Alexa out of his mind. Ever since she had disappeared, her image had been in his thoughts, stopping him from thinking clearly, preventing him from sleeping.

In fact, if he was being honest, she'd been in his head from the first moment they had met. Petra might have described her as dull and dowdy, but there had been something about her that had caught on his senses and wouldn't let go. Even when he'd thought her cold and stiffly distant, he had been intrigued by her. The woman who had come to tell him about her sister's disappearance had been someone else again, the one he held in his arms as they had danced another person entirely. Then there was the woman whose hair he had released until it fell in a cloud of soft silk about her face, whose eyes had glistened in the moonlight as her body strained towards him, whose mouth had practically begged for his kisses until he had thought that he would groan aloud with the strain of withholding them. But it was the woman he had taken to bed who had eclipsed them all.

That woman had haunted his nights, keeping him from sleep, or, if he did slide into a doze, had made his slumber restless and uneasy as heated erotic images walked through his dreams, murmuring his name, offering her mouth to his, her body opening to his caress.

And when he had woken, sweating and shaken, with his heart racing at twice its normal speed, he had found himself hard and aching, his body aroused by the night's imaginings and clamouring for the release it needed. A release that Alexa's flight had forced him to deny it.

But not any more. In the moment that she had opened the door, he had known exactly why he was here. The shoes were no real excuse; revenge might be part of it but sheer physical craving was more, so much more. Seeing her as he had never seen her before, with the soft cherry-red jumper and the tightly clinging jeans emphasising gentle curves, her hair tumbling in loose waves, her beautiful skin touched with just the smallest trace of make-up, he had felt his heart kick hard in his chest. The fierce sting of hunger had started up lower down in his body, so strongly that it had been an effort to speak and not just to reach out and drag her into his arms, kissing her until they were both senseless with need and passion.

'I'm here to finish what we started,' he declared, the twist of sexual hunger making his voice raw and rough. 'I've come for you.'

CHAPTER NINE

'COME FOR...'

Alexa couldn't believe what she had heard. Panic was buzzing inside her head, making her thoughts reel, so she was sure that she hadn't actually caught what he had said. That he couldn't have said...

He just couldn't have said 'I've come for you.'

Could he?

But Santos stood there, big and dark and dangerous, with his scarred hand raised to unfasten the buttons of his heavy coat. And with that gleam in his eyes, the taunting one that she had come, through painful experience, to recognise as meaning trouble for someone—and in this case that someone was very definitely her.

Even if he was just teasing then it was a cold-blooded, wicked teasing, one that made her nerves twist in apprehension and lifted the hairs on the back of her neck in a way that made her shiver inwardly.

'What do you mean, you've come for me? There's nothing for you here. Nothing about me that you could want or can have.'

'Are you so sure of that?' Santos shrugged himself out of his coat and tossed it aside so that it landed on one of the two-seater settees that furnished the room, the navy cashmere heavy and dark against the soft pale grey cotton that covered it.

'Of course…'

That fiendish gleam had brightened disturbingly and the faint lift of one straight dark brow in cynical enquiry was more worrying that any more blatant threat.

'You're forgetting something,' he drawled softly, the fascinating accent deepening on the silky words so that in spite of herself Alexa couldn't suppress the recognition of how attractive that voice was, how it tugged at her sensuality, sending prickles of awareness down her spine. She didn't want to find anything about this man attractive but she just couldn't deny the almost shocking appeal he had for her.

'Oh, really—and just what is it that I've forgotten?'

'That your family owes me a wife. The wedding that never was,' Santos elaborated coolly when her head went back in shock, her eyes widening in disbelief and she struggled to accept that he had actually said what she thought she had heard. And, even worse, that he had meant it.

'My *sister's* wedding!' she protested. 'She was the one who was supposed to marry you.'

'Exactly.'

It was crisp and cold as the hail that was whirling outside, blown wildly up against the window and forming a thick curtain so that it was almost impossible to see through to the garden beyond.

'But—how can my family owe you a wife—owe you anything? I know that Natalie broke her promise to marry you but surely you aren't going to—'

'There was more to it than that. So much more.'

'More in what way?'

'Oh, come on, Alexa…'

That now familiar arrogant gesture with his hand dismissed the question as not even worth bothering with, never mind answering. And if she had thought that the wild storm outside had looked cold then it was as nothing when compared to the ice in his eyes as they blazed at her across the room, chilling her blood so that she feared that she would never, ever be warm again.

'Let us not play games here. We both know what I mean.'

'I have no idea what you're talking about.'

'It would be better if we were straight with each other.'

'I don't know how to be anything but straight because I don't know what you mean!'

It was impossible to control the tremble in her voice, impossible to stop it rising in fear and uncertainty. She was still struggling so hard to come to terms with what he had said and to work out just how he might actually mean it.

I've come for you...

Your family owes me a wife.

The two phrases couldn't be connected—they just couldn't. And there really was no way that they could mean what she feared—that he had come for her because he believed that her family owed him a wife and she was the wife he had in mind.

No, it was impossible. She couldn't believe it. And yet there had been that appalling proposition he had flung in her face on the evening of the wedding.

And did she mean feared—or something else entirely?

She had been unaware of the way that she was shaking her head in frantic denial until she heard Santos's voice again, cold and incisive, cutting through the blur of confusion in her brain.

'No? Are you saying no, we should not be straight with each other or no, let us not play games?'

'I'm saying no, this can't be happening. No, it doesn't make sense—none of it.'

'Why not?'

There was no way she could escape the fierce, intensely focused burn of his watchful eyes. They were fixed on her face as she spoke, observing every tiny flicker of emotion across her features, every change of mood, every sign of uncertainty and confusion. Watching her so coldly and unwaveringly that she felt as if she were some small, defenceless harvest mouse, cowering in a corner of a field, vulnerable and exposed and praying desperately that the cruel, hunting eyes of a hovering bird of prey would somehow pass over her and let her escape.

But Santos was clearly in no mood to ease up on her. He had no intention of letting her get away.

'To me it makes perfect sense. What is wrong with what I am saying? Why can it not make sense?' Santos enquired with a softness that stunned her as it was so much in contrast to the burn of his gaze.

'Because there is no way you can claim that you want me as your wife.'

It must all be a pretence. Some sort of dark, twisted game. One that he was playing deliberately to make her squirm, to make her burn up in embarrassment.

'No way that you can say that you came here for that.'

'And why not, hmm?' Santos shot back.

'Because—because I'm not Natalie!'

'Do you think I don't know that? And do you not realise that that is exactly what makes this arrangement so much better in my eyes?'

Had he just paid her a huge compliment, or flung another insult in her face? Alexa couldn't decide and her brain felt too bruised and muddled to work it out.

'How can I want you as my wife? Why not? I told you this before and you reacted as if I had thrown a live snake into your face. As if I had given you the worst possible insult.'

'You had.'

Anger at the memory of that appalling moment brought a new strength to Alexa's voice, bringing her chin up defiantly, hazel eyes blazing into his cold silvery ones.

'My proposal of marriage was an insult to you?' He actually sounded shocked, as if *she* was the one who had insulted *him*.

'It wasn't so much a proposal as a demand that I could take Natalie's place. One Montague sister was as good as another, you said.'

And was that really why he was here now? To suggest once again that she could replace her sister as his bride? Her brain threatened to blow a fuse simply at the thought.

But would he have come all this way if she was simply a replacement? Or was she being totally weak and stupid to allow herself to dream that perhaps, after all, she had made some impact on him? That he hadn't been able to forget her as she had found it totally impossible to get the image of his dark, stunning face, those pale eyes and the beautifully accented voice out of her mind.

'I was angry when I said that. In that I was wrong.'

Santos's response brought her head up sharply, shocked hazel eyes looking into cool grey ones.

'Is that meant to be an apology?'

'It is the truth. I never wanted your sister as I want you. And if she had run to some strange little cottage in the wilds of Yorkshire, then I would have thought twice about following her.'

'It's not a strange…' Alexa began but then the realisation of just what he had said sank into her numbed brain. 'Is that the truth too?'

'Why should I lie to you, *belleza*? That is exactly the point.'

His gaze still held hers as he spoke, his eyes so deep and clear that she felt they were like a still, smooth pool in which she risked drowning, going in over her head completely.

'And precisely just what point is that?'

The look Santos turned on her questioned the justification for her fury, seeming to wonder just why she was overreacting in this way, which of course only added fuel to the fire, making her breath hiss in between clenched teeth, her eyes sparking fury as they glared into his.

'I would have thought that was obvious.'

'Not to me it isn't! So tell me exactly what *point* you were trying to make.'

Santos moved to fling himself down onto one of the small settees, pushed both hands through the dark sleekness of his hair as he lounged back against the multicoloured cushions on the settee, infuriatingly at his ease.

'In Spain you said there was no way you could marry me because we had never even kissed,' Santos pointed out with exasperating calm. 'I simply put that right. But I suspected—knew—that there would be more to it than that. And I was proved right.'

Alexa feared that her head might actually burst open under the pressure of the outrage and fury that was pounding through her. She could have very little doubt as to just what sort of 'more' to it there was in what Santos was implying.

'I told you that I never slept with Natalie and you asked—'

'If you believed that if she'd once experienced your love-making she'd never want to get away from you. That she would have become so addicted that she'd have to stay around for more,' Alexa put in angrily when he hesitated, seeming not to be able to remember just what she had said.

Too late she realised that she had fallen head first right into the trap that she hadn't even noticed he was digging for her.

'I never thought that would be the case with Natalie,' Santos drawled, actually having the nerve to smile up at her as he spoke. 'But I knew how it would be with you. That if I touched you, you would go up in flames.'

Alexa's only response was a furious hiss, like a hostile snake. She tried to find something coherent to say but every single line escaped her and there was no way any words would form.

'And I was right. Which means that I've made it so much easier for you.'

'Easier!' The word exploded from Alexa's tongue, all the

anger, the disbelief she was feeling rolled up into the three short syllables. 'Easier, precisely how?'

Santos struggled against the smile that tugged at the corner of his mouth. He knew it would only incense her further, her fury giving away just how much he had got to her, which was exactly what he wanted. He wanted her off balance—on edge—just as he was feeling right now.

There was no way he was going to let her know just how he too had gone up in flames that night; the hell of frustration he'd been going through ever since. The hell he was still experiencing as his aroused body yelled a furious protest at being held back like this, at being deprived of the pleasure and satisfaction it had been anticipating all the way here. The pleasure and satisfaction that had been in his mind from the moment that Alexa had opened the door. Or even before that. As he had driven up the narrow, rutted road that led from the village to this cottage, the image of Alexa that had haunted his dreams and driven him to distraction in the day had been there in his mind, taunting him, tempting him, arousing him.

And once he had seen her in the flesh again, looking so appealing in the casual red sweater and denim jeans, her hair a soft cloud around her face, he had known that he could never leave again without having her in his bed, without knowing that slender body intimately once more. The problem was that he suspected that 'once more' would never, ever be enough and the way that his arousal nagged at him reinforced that idea in a painful way.

'You know how the sex was between us—how it will be again. And so you can see that our marriage will be good for both of us—'

'It will not be good for me—for either of us—because we are *not getting married*! I will not just replace Natalie as your bride.'

'No,' Santos agreed with feeling, knowing that he had shocked her by doing so, leaving her gaping faintly in surprise.

Feeling he might be more comfortable standing up, he got to his feet, that temptation to smile surfacing again as he saw the way her eyes sparked and she edged away like a nervous horse. If only she realised just how much she was giving away by her unthinking action.

'You will not *just replace* Natalie in any way because I never felt this way about her. My relationship with her never had this heat, or this intensity.'

Oh, how she wished that he would stop saying things like that, Alexa told herself. She didn't want to hear them, didn't want to believe them.

And yet they were the things she most wanted to hear in the whole world.

The thought that a man—*this* man—this devastatingly handsome, stunning man—might actually prefer her to her sister, that she might have an effect on him that all Natalie's blonde beauty had never managed, made her head spin and her nerves fizz with purely feminine excitement.

'We'd be good together, Alexa.'

Hastily she dragged her weak thoughts back from the enticing path they were tempted to follow. A path that might lead to some immediate pleasure, a sort of satisfaction, but one that would never last and that would only leave her so much more lost and bereft when it was over. She had always vowed that she would never lurch into some half-formed or just plain bad idea of a liaison simply because of the attraction she felt.

But oh, if there was ever a man who could tempt her to go back on that resolve then that man was Santos Cordero.

As he stood before her, black hair mussed, silvery eyes gleaming, his half-fastened shirt revealing part of the olive-toned chest she had once caressed and kissed, the man was temptation personified. He was the handsome, irresistible, seductive snake in the Garden of Eden. And he had made no secret of how much he wanted her.

Dear heaven, but she was tempted. Just for once she wanted to let go of all common sense, throw off the restraints she had imposed on herself and enjoy the fizzing, burning, wild, crazy excitement a hot-blooded, purely sexual affair could bring.

But even as she thought them, the words *wild* and *crazy* hit home, forcing her to reconsider. Wild and crazy was not part of her make-up and never would be.

'Good together in bed maybe—but that's no reason to get married!'

'Is it not? To me it seems like one of the best reasons there is.'

'But we don't even like each other—except in that way.'

'Does that matter?'

Santos shrugged off her protest with a lazy lift of his shoulders.

'I know many married couples who openly detest each other and they stay together because of their lifestyle and the fact that one partner is providing what the other one enjoys. At least we would have the passion as well.'

'And that would be enough for you?'

'It would be a damn good place to start.'

To start.

No, she was not going to allow herself to read anything into that. Hadn't he stated openly and bluntly that he didn't believe in love; that he never had and never would?

'Why don't you believe in love?' she asked suddenly, unable to fight the burning curiosity that overcame her, though she was almost as stunned as he looked to hear her actually voice the question out loud.

But whatever surprise Santos had felt he very soon recovered from, the look of shock fading rapidly from his pale eyes to be replaced by a coldly cynical scorn.

'I have seen no evidence that it exists.'

'Oh, come on!' There was no way she could let him get away

with that. No one could get to the age of thirty-three without ever seeing love in some shape or form. 'You must have!'

'Must I?'

The enquiry was so calm, so matter-of-fact, almost throwaway, that it sent a shivery sensation over her skin, warning her that she was dealing with something here that she had never encountered in her life before.

'Well, surely your parents…?'

Santos's response was a snarl of such bitter, humourless laughter that it made her blood run cold just to hear it.

'Definitely not my parents. There too was a couple who did not need to love each other in order to create another life.'

'Your mother must have loved you,' Alexa hazarded, her heart suddenly seeming to beat high up in a throat that was tight with tension, making it almost impossible to force the question out past the constriction.

The icily burning look that Santos turned on her from those amazing eyes threatened to shrivel her to dust right where she stood and it took all her mental courage to stay where she was and not turn tail and run.

'Even if my mother had stayed around long enough to get to know me, I doubt if she would ever have felt anything like the way that love is described in fiction or fairy stories. To be strictly honest, I would find it hard to believe that she would have felt anything at all.'

'But she was your mother!'

'She gave birth to me, *es todo*.'

If there was any feeling behind the cold, set mask that was Santos's face, he was not letting it show. His features might have been carved from marble for all the emotion they revealed, and the glittering eyes had turned as cloudy and opaque as the blank eyeballs of ancient statues.

'And—your father?'

Alexa didn't really want to ask the question; she had the

nasty feeling that she wasn't going to like the answer one little bit. No one became as cynical as Santos obviously was without good reason, and she was beginning to see that he had more reasons than she had ever suspected.

'My father?'

The sound of Santos's laughter made her shrink away inside it was so cold and brutal, and she almost expected to see the words splinter into shards right there on the carpet in front of her.

'I doubt if *mi madre* even knew who my father was. He could have been any one of a dozen possible candidates. Whoever he was, he certainly did not want to take care of a young boy, either.'

There was no self-pity in his voice, nothing in it that seemed to ask for any sympathy. Instead he maintained that appalling matter-of-fact tone that made her wince at every word. The stiffness of his long back, the careful blanking off of all expression in his eyes made her want to reach out and touch him, take his hand in hers in an expression of compassion. But even as the thought crossed her mind the immediate recognition of just what his response would be chased it away again.

He would hate it if she showed any concern for him, and would probably repulse her gesture with a brusque one, though he was so armoured against any sympathy that perhaps it wouldn't touch him at all. But it was the fear of what any touch might do to her that held her back most strongly. After the incendiary effects of Santos's caresses and kisses once before, she wasn't prepared to risk that all over again. She felt as if she had barely escaped unscathed as it was and the danger of putting her hand into the fire all over again was more than she could bear.

Which reminded her only too sharply of just why he was here in the first place. The cold-blooded declaration he had made on his arrival.

I've come for you...

She could well believe that he was callous enough to do just that. The man who had declared so openly that he didn't believe in love and who had only wanted a dynastic marriage to a member of the Montague family—any daughter of the Montague family, it seemed.

'It doesn't matter how good our one night together was, it was one night and it's over, I have no intention of repeating it ever again.'

The look in his eyes, the faint lift of an eyebrow questioned her statement but she ignored it and plunged on.

'I will not marry you. I don't want anything to do with you.'

'Liar,' he said softly. 'Look at what happened when I kissed you.'

'What happened then was lust—it had nothing to do with love.'

'And you need love before you marry?'

'Yes! Yes, I do!'

'Well, forgive me, *carina*, but I can't offer you that. But I can offer you a great deal—'

'And I don't want it. I don't want anything from you. What?' she asked as she saw his proud head go back as if in shock, black brows drawing together sharply in a dark frown. 'What have I said?'

'If that is the truth, then I suggest that you talk to your father about this.'

'My father—why?'

She was thoroughly confused now. There was no reason at all why he should bring her father into this.

'If you really don't know then he will tell you. It will come better from him.'

'I have no intention of talking to my father. Nothing he can say will make me marry you.'

'Are you sure of that?'

'Positive.'

Santos seemed to need a couple of seconds to absorb what she had said, and for once his pale eyes were not clear and cold but clouded with something she didn't understand.

'Do you know why I was going to marry Natalie?'

'Of course—you wanted marriage to found your dynasty of Cordero heirs.'

That realisation hit home like a blow to her chest, twisting something sharp and deadly in her heart. The image of a child that had Santos as its father, a boy with his dark strength or a girl with a softer, feminine version of that jet-black hair and stunning eyes, floated in her head. Children who would not have learned his cold cynicism and come to deny the idea of love. And children through whom their father might come to see that there was some emotion that he had never known, never understood in the rest of his life.

'And you still do—but you can't force me to marry you!'

'I promise you that I don't intend to use force. But you will marry me.'

'No way! Never!'

The smile that flickered across his lips made her blood run cold, and, even worse, it forced her to look at what she had said, hear it again in her thoughts, and catch the shrillness, the edge of panic in her voice that gave away so much more than was comfortable.

'Is there not a saying about never saying never?' Santos drawled easily, flashing her that smile once more, but this time there was no charm in it. This time his eyes were pure ice and the curve of his lips was a promise of retribution if she didn't do things his way.

'There might be, but I think you'll find that it doesn't apply to me.'

'Talk to your father, Alexa.'

It was low, almost soft, but there was a sombre severity

about his tone that pulled her up sharp, making her look deep into his face, trying to read something of what was going through his mind in those unfathomable pale eyes. But Santos was giving nothing away. Instead it was as if a heavy metal shutter had clanged to behind his eyes, cutting off everything from her and concealing his thoughts from her totally.

'Just what is going on here?'

But Santos simply shook his head, his beautiful mouth shut tight over any possible explanation.

'All right…'

Backed into a corner, she knew there was no other way she could react. But she wasn't going to let him enjoy his triumph.

'All right, I'll talk to my father but not now—not with you standing over me like some avenging angel. If I have to do this then I'll do it in privacy—with you out of the house. Go on…' she pushed when he didn't respond, didn't move. 'I want you to leave—get out of my house…'

Just what she would do if he refused to budge, she had no idea. A scary, impossible image of her trying to actually physically move him, pushing him towards the door, flared in her head, making her shudder inwardly at the mere thought. But then, just as she was afraid she might actually have to try it he lifted his shoulders in a dismissive shrug.

'OK,' he said casually. 'I'll leave—for now. I need to check in to my hotel and there are a couple of business calls I need to make. But I'll be back.'

The implied threat in the last three words, and the way that he emphasised them, pale, gleaming gaze fixed on her face as if searching for something that only he could see, made her nerves jump.

'You'll leave and you'll not come back, not until I say you can! If I say you can. When I've talked to my father, if I think we still need to talk, I'll give you a call.'

Did she really think she was having any effect at all on him?

He might have agreed to leave, but that was because it suited him, for now. His face was closed off again so that she had no idea if she was getting through to him at all. The truth was that she doubted very much that she was. Santos would do things his own way and only that way. He was only going along with what she said because she was doing what he actually wanted her to do. The feeling of having been manipulated, out-manoeuvred by a master was a nasty, creeping one along her skin. Just what would her father have to tell her when she got in touch with him?

Santos was shrugging himself back into his heavy over-coat, pushing his hand into one of the pockets and pulling out a small silver case. Flipping it open, he pulled out a slip of white embossed card and held it out to her.

'My mobile number,' he explained when Alexa could only stare in blank confusion. 'You'll need it when you ring me.'

When, Alexa noted. Not if. He was totally sure of himself, and of her, totally in control. She had never felt more like a stiff, wooden puppet, dancing at the command of the man who pulled the strings.

In a moment of petty rebellion she refused to take the card he offered, her chin coming up defiantly as her eyes locked with his until he gave a small bark of harsh laughter and tossed it down onto the arm of the settee.

'You'll need it,' he said implacably. 'Call me.'

He was turning away as he spoke, fastening his coat and turning his collar up high against the weather outside. Weather that was getting worse by the second if the wail of the wind howling round the cottage was anything to go by. It seemed amazing to Alexa that she hadn't noticed the way it sounded before, but then she had been—distracted was all she would admit to herself.

She hesitated over insisting that Santos should leave when she saw just what conditions were like outside as she opened the door. Not only had the wind increased in both speed and power, buffeting the trees so that they swayed wildly and dangerously in its force, but the rain was lashing down too and some of it was in the form of icy hailstones, battering the few straggly plants in her garden.

'Are you sure you'll be OK?'

'What's this, Alexa?' Santos mocked. 'Concern? I'm a big boy…'

'I know you are,' Alexa snapped, unsettled by both concern for his safety and the fact that she felt it, her stomach clenching unexpectedly at the thought of him having to drive in these appalling conditions. 'Big enough and ugly enough. But I wouldn't put a dog out in this.'

'I'll survive.'

He shrugged off her concern in a way that, strangely, only made her feel so much worse. From wanting him gone, needing the peace of her home to herself, free from his unsettling presence so that she could contact her father and find out just what was going on, she had veered towards a feeling that she should not let him go. What if something happened to him? The night was closing in and the road towards the village was very badly lit. Its surface was pitted and rough and, even if he knew its twists and turns well as she did, she feared that driving it in these conditions would be an ordeal.

'Don't go,' she said suddenly, spinning round to face Santos, only to realise that he had already left her side, that he was opening the car door, sliding into the driving seat.

For a moment she considered running after him. She even lifted her hand to wave, to beg him to stop, but the roar of the car's powerful engine had her dropping it down to her side again.

Santos wouldn't stay to please her, to calm her fears. Why would he want to? And wouldn't admitting to those worries give him more of a hold over her, knowing that she cared? And so she forced herself to stand there and watch as Santos put the car into gear and set off down the road away from the cottage.

It was unnerving seeing the way that the vehicle was pounded by the fearsome winds, once even knocked to the side by the force of the gale, but Santos quickly regained control. A moment later he had reached a turn in the road, and even the rear lights of the car had disappeared from sight. As she watched them go, another wild flurry of rain and hail lashed at her face, making her shiver in miserable response. It really was a vile night, and somehow with Santos gone it seemed darker, colder and bleaker than ever.

Talk to your father, Alexa. Santos's voice sounded in her head, reminding her of what she must do, and with another shiver, one she wasn't at all sure was completely physical, she turned and hurried back inside, letting the door swing to behind her as she moved to pick up the phone.

CHAPTER TEN

DID ALEXA MONTAGUE really not know what was going on, or was she playing some more complicated, carefully planned game along with the rest of her family?

The question nagged at Santos's thoughts as he drove away from the cottage, distracting him dangerously from the control of his car. He really needed all his concentration in the appalling weather conditions.

But in spite of the fact that he knew he should think of driving and nothing else it was impossible to stop his thoughts drifting back over the time he had spent in the cottage, and the images of Alexa as she had been then.

He wanted to recall the things she had said, how she had spoken them, and most importantly how she had looked as she'd reacted to him or answered his questions. He needed to be able to interpret her facial expressions, her body language, to try to understand just what was going on here, but the problem was that the memories he needed were not the ones he could recall most easily.

Instead, the images that flooded his mind were ones from that night in Seville, sensuous, erotic, doubly distracting. In his mind's eye he could see again the way that Alexa had looked when he kissed her. He could have sworn that he could still taste the essence of her on his lips, and if he licked them to ease their sudden dryness it was as if he had only just lifted his mouth from hers, a memory that set his heart pounding and made the hunger of sensual need clutch at his loins.

Once again he lived through the moment of looking down at her as she lay under him on the bed, seeing the long strands of her soft brown hair spread out on the pillows around her head. Her eyes had been the deep dark green of a mossy pool, her lips blushing pink in response to the pressure of his kisses. The soft scent of her skin had been all around him, blending with some delicately floral perfume that still lingered in his nostrils even though he was already so far away from her. And under the weight of his own body, her soft curves had been a warm, sensual delight, her breasts just perfectly filling his hands

'*Maldito sea*, no!'

Savagely he cursed aloud, dragging his thoughts back to the present and the hellish road he was trying to negotiate in the pitch-darkness. Even the beam of his headlights was blurred and distorted by the lashing rain and the savage hailstorm.

And the focus of his thoughts was no clearer. He wanted to be able to think without letting sensual hunger distract him from what mattered. But the truth was that where Alexa was concerned there was no hope of thinking of anything other than the aching sexual hunger she woke in him simply by existing. Even now he was hot and hard just thinking of her, remembering the way she had responded to him, her soft moans when he had touched her, the way she had given herself up to his caresses.

But had he let that primitive need, that most basic of male appetites, blind him to anything else? Was she truly as innocent as she sometimes seemed, or just pretending to be unaware of the set-up that the supposed wedding had been? And if so, was she—?

'Hell and damnation!'

The raw, ragged creaking sound alerted him just in time.

At the very last possible minute he saw the way that a large tree on the edge of the road was waving more wildly in the wind than all the others. The ominous noise came again, louder this time, audible even above the wail of the wind, and with a terrible wrenching, splintering sound the great trunk split apart and started to fall.

'*Madre de Dios!*'

Fingers clenched hard over the steering wheel until his knuckles showed white, he swung it sharply to the left, slamming his foot down on the brakes hard at the same time. He could only pray that he had reacted fast enough as a sound like roaring, deafening thunder crashed through the air.

Alexa pressed the off switch on the phone and set it back down in its holder with a sigh. This was the second time she'd got the answering machine's automated voice asking her to 'leave a message after the tone' and there was no way that she could say what she needed to say to her father in an impersonal recording. The best thing she could do was to leave a request for him to ring her back as soon as he got in from wherever he'd gone.

And she'd hope and pray that that would be soon. She had very little belief that Santos would stay away for long. Or that he would wait for her to phone him to say he should come back. Santos Cordero was not a man who waited around for anyone's permission to do anything he wanted to do.

The thought had barely faded from her mind when the front door was pushed open suddenly, making her jump like a startled cat, and, as if conjured up by her reflections, Santos himself strode into the hallway in a flurry of wind and hail.

'What are you doing here?'

Irritation at his blatant disregard of her demand that he should not return until she asked him to warred with the unwanted but uncontrollable leap of her heart at the sight of him to create a volatile mood in which she didn't know what she should be feeling and why.

'Getting out of the wind and rain,' was the laconic reply as he raked one hand through the black hair that had been blown over his forehead, pushing it back away from his face.

The howling gale had messed the normally sleek black hair wildly and sparkled it with raindrops and the cold had made his skin glow, the silvery eyes gleaming brilliantly. He had never looked so vividly, so vibrantly alive and the sight of him sent a rush of blood through every vein, bringing with it a flurry of memories of how it had felt to be in his arms, his kisses on her mouth, his hands caressing her skin. She could feel the hot blood flood her cheeks and prayed he would take it as being put there by anger at his reappearance.

'I told you not to come back unless I phoned you. I didn't phone you.'

'I'm well aware of that…' Santos began but, launched on this mood of indignation, Alexa found that she much preferred it to the wildly fluctuating feelings she had had as he walked through the door and so she let it carry her onwards, speaking over his words without really listening.

'So what are you doing back here? Walking into the house as if you owned the place. I thought you had things to do— phone calls to make…'

'I do!' Santos declared in exasperation when she finally drew enough breath to let him get a word in edgeways. 'And believe me I would have left if I could. Trailing back here in this gale was not exactly my first choice of how to do things.'

'Then why—?'

'I had no choice, Alexa!' he flung at her coldly. 'There was nothing else I could do!'

'Nothing else? Do you think I'll believe that? When you've come sneaking back here…'

'I did not sneak.'

'…riding roughshod over what I said I wanted—probably with some other plan to get me into your bed. Do you think I can't see through you? Oh, come on—'

But she never completed the sentence, breaking off in shock as Santos lurched forward to grab hold of her arm.

'No, you come on!'

Before she quite knew what was happening he had grabbed her coat from the hooks on the wall and wrapped it round her.

'You have your shoes on? Good.'

'Santos…'

She struggled to pull away but he held her close, huddling her against the protection of his chest with one arm as with his free hand he wrenched open the door and headed out into the fury of the gale.

'Santos!' Alexa protested as the icy winds bruised her face, making her flinch back.

But a moment later the discomfort eased as she found that he had manoeuvred the hard bulk of his body so that it shielded her from the worst of the elements, pulling part of his coat around her too as extra protection. She was snug and safe in a special cocoon, one in which the heat of his body reached her even through her clothes, and the scent of his skin surrounded her, warm and musky against the bite of the freezing wind.

In the space of a couple of heartbeats she had forgotten her discomfort, forgotten her annoyance, forgotten everything but the wonderful safe, secure feeling she had being held so close to him, his arm around her shoulders, his chest against her arm, his hip rubbing hers as he strode furiously down the pitted road in the direction in which she had seen him drive just a short time before.

Another couple of moments more and that safe and secure feeling had given way to something new and very different. In spite of the weather she was almost too warm in her cocoon, her body heated by the heavy pulse of her own blood as it thundered in primitive response to the touch of his hand, the movement of his powerful body. The memory of all that hard maleness crushing her beneath him on the bed, the burning force of his erection pressed into her pelvis, made her mouth dry and blurred her eyes so that she had to be grateful for Santos's control, the surefooted way he guided her along the gloomy path. The impulse to stop, to turn in those strong arms, and drag his handsome head down to hers, to crush her lips to his in a hungry, yearning kiss, was almost overwhelming and she actually welcomed the lash of the rain in her face as it forced her to keep a hold on reality.

'There.'

Santos came to an abrupt halt, jolting her out of her heated daydream, sending her sensual thoughts flying as he flung out a hand in an emphatic gesture to draw her attention to the scene before her.

'See…'

'What am I looking at—what—? Oh!'

Her question choked off on a cry of shock and distress as she saw what was before her; what he wanted her to see.

The car in which Santos had driven off now stood at a crazy angle, half on the road and half on the grass verge at the edge of it, where it had obviously swerved violently to avoid something. And it was the something that brought the distress into her voice, making her eyes widen in stunned horror as they focused on the broken, splintered trunk of an enormous tree that had come crashing down in the storm and now lay right across the road, blocking the way completely. Several of the smaller branches had broken off and were scattered around the place, and one large, heavy one had actually crashed into the side-window of the vehicle, splintering the glass where it had landed.

'That's why you—you couldn't leave—you crashed.'

Her voice quavered badly on the last word. Somehow actually saying it made it all the more real, all the more disturbing and it brought back the dreadful feeling she had had when she had seen him drive away, the fear that something might happen—something like this.

She found she was trembling all over and not from the cold. Not any more.

Just looking at the car she realised what a narrow escape Santos had had. Another metre or two further forward and his car would have been directly in the line of the tree as it fell. The weight of the huge trunk would have flattened the vehicle—and its driver. The thought of Santos with his strong body crushed and broken sent fearful shudders running through her, her legs seeming to turn to water.

'Are you all right?'

In the shadowy night she turned to him, trying to recall how he had looked when he had arrived back at the house. Dishevelled, windswept, wet—but uninjured.

He *had* been unhurt, hadn't he? She had been too taken aback, too irritated to look closely. She wouldn't have noticed if there had been anything wrong.

'Santos—are you hurt? Did the tree…?'

The horror of the possibilities overcame her again and hot tears stung at her eyes so that she had to blink furiously as she tried to focus on his handsome face. Acting purely on instinct, she lifted a hand, fingers shaking, and pressed it to his cheek, needing to feel his warmth, know his strength, and know that nothing terrible had happened to him.

'Tell me you're not hurt.'

'I'm fine… Truly I am—I got out of the car just in time. Alexa…'

His hand, warm and strong and comforting, came up to cover hers where it lay against his cheek, pressing it softly so that she was trapped between the two different types of skin.

The hardness of his palm and the softer flesh of his face where the evening's growth of stubble was already starting to show and it pricked at her own palm with a faint roughness that made her fingers want to curve tight against it.

She needed to touch him, needed to feel the strength and the warmth of him under her hands, skin against skin, life against life. Just the thought that he might have been injured—worse, that she might have lost him before she had fully realised what he could mean to her was so terrible, so terrifying that she couldn't control her reaction to it.

'Alexa?' Santos's tone was soft, concerned but slightly rough at the edges as if he didn't quite know how to pitch it. But that wasn't possible, Santos always knew just what he was doing—he never opened his mouth without thinking. 'Alexa, I'm fine—nothing happened. Nothing hit me.'

Perhaps if he hadn't been gentle, if that hand that covered hers hadn't curved closer, pressed a little harder, she might have held it together. But his tenderness was just too much, breaking through the shattered barriers of her control, destroying them completely. From somewhere deep inside tears welled up again, pressing at the backs of her eyes but refusing to fall. Instead, she had to let her feelings out some way and so she launched herself forward, capturing his mouth with her own and pressing hungry, emotional kisses onto his warm lips.

'Alexa!'

Her name was a rough, shaken sound in his throat and for just the space of a single heartbeat as she felt him stiffen, strong muscles tautening, she feared that he was going to draw back, push her away. But then his whole mood changed, his mouth softening against her, his arms enfolding her in a new and very different way as he gathered her close and returned kiss for kiss, his hands lacing into her hair to cup the fine bones of her skull and hold her just where he wanted her. Where his hungry mouth could have the most devastating effect.

For several long, heated moments they were oblivious to the storm that raged around them, only aware of the storm of sensation that was building up inside. But then on a long, low moan, another wilder, blisteringly cold flurry of hail whirled round them, lifting their hair on their heads, making their coats fly up around them and slowly, reluctantly, Santos lifted his head, drew back.

'No…' Alexa muttered a protest, reaching for him again, still with her eyes half-closed.

'Alexa,' Santos reproved softly, 'we will freeze if we stay out here.'

Freeze? In the privacy of her own thoughts, Alexa questioned the truth of his comment. She had never felt so hot in her life, so bone-deep, her blood pounding, totally warm from the inside out, and even the whirling wind and the lashing rain were having no effect on her.

'No…' she murmured again and felt rather than saw the shake of his dark head as she heard the low laughter that escaped him.

'Yes, *querida*—already you are soaked… We must make our way back to the house.'

Querida, she registered. He had used that word before but on a blackly ironical note. Now suddenly his tone seemed to have softened, almost as if he meant it, as if he was concerned by her reaction. As if he truly was calling her *darling*… Her head was spinning with the delight of it.

'Then let's go back.' The thickness in her throat made the words as huskily provocative as she planned them to be. 'And get warm.'

Was her heart really thundering as heavily as it seemed? Or was that just the sound of the wind sending heavy branches thudding to the ground or the rain pounding on the cottage roof? She didn't know or care. Her only thought was to get back into the cottage, to close the door on the world and shut herself in with Santos so that they could be alone together.

She was not even sure if she was walking, if her feet were actually touching the ground as they hurried towards the tiny house. Santos had her held so close to his side, his grip around her waist so tight that she was sure he was carrying her part of the way rather than letting her manage it herself. And in the moment that they stumbled through the front door he caught her to him and crushed her mouth with his before he swung her up into his arms as he had done on the night of the wedding and carried her into the hall, kicking the door to behind him as he headed for the stairs.

'First on the left…' Alexa managed against his neck, the slightly salty taste of his skin making her heart skip a couple of ragged beats as she savoured it against her tongue.

'*Si*…'

Her room was dark and shadowy but the curtains were still open at the window and the moon gave enough light for Santos to see his way to the bed, taking her with him and tumbling her gently down onto the covers. But when she reached for him to pull him down with her he pulled away from her and turned away.

'Santos!'

It was a cry of protest and distress, the loss of the heat and strength of his body too much to bear.

'What…?'

'I was looking for a towel…' The roughness of his voice told clearly of the struggle he too was having for control. 'You need to dry your—'

'I need no such thing!'

It was impossible to tell if she was breathless with laughter, with the cold or with the deep frustration of the need that was eating away at her.

'Santos, all I need is you! You can warm me best!'

For a second she thought that she was going to have to get up and drag him onto the bed with her but before she could move he had swung round again, flinging off his coat and throwing it down onto the floor in the same moment as he came down beside her, gathering her up into his arms once more.

If she had ever been cold, then Alexa couldn't remember it now. Her whole body was on fire, burning up with need and the heated arousal Santos's touch woke in her. And that heat didn't fade as he stripped her clothes from her, hungry fingers occasionally fumbling with uncharacteristic clumsiness as he dealt with buttons and zips, the clasp on her bra. The truth was that every touch of his hands, every brush of his fingertips against her skin made her pulse kick up another notch, sending more blood throbbing in her veins, molten and hungry, a yearning desire uncoiling low down in her body, making her damp and aching between her legs.

Her mouth clamped to his, Alexa's own fingers were rough with need as she tugged at his shirt, sighing her satisfaction as he shrugged it off and tossed it aside. At last she could trail her fingers over the heated satin of his skin, tangle her fingers in the soft crispness of body hair, inhale the musky scent of his aroused body, a perfume so heady and intoxicating that it made her feel close to swooning in heavy, erotic pleasure.

'I want you,' she muttered against his chest, letting her tongue slide out and taste him, circling the small, dark nub of his nipple, feeling it harden underneath her kisses. 'Oh, dear heaven, Santos, how I…'

The words broke off on a long, gasping moan of pleasure as he matched her caresses with his own. Taking each breast in one hand, he cupped and stroked them, squeezing softly, lifting first one and then the other to his mouth, slicking his tongue across the yearning, sensitive tip, then blowing softly on the moistened bud, sending stinging, tingling sensations arrowing along every nerve, tugging at the most sensitive spot at the juncture of her thighs.

Her jeans felt roughly constricting, far too tight, so that she moved restlessly on the plain white quilt, brushing her pelvis against the swollen, heated evidence of his desire until he groaned a hungry response.

'You witch!' he muttered thickly. 'Temptress—tormentor…'

But even as he spoke he was freeing her from the confinement of her clothes, smoothing his hands along the slender lines of her legs, over the softness of her inner thighs, slipping through the cluster of curls to caress her intimately.

'Santos…'

His name was a sigh of surrender and need and she opened herself up to him, clutching her hands in his hair and arching her back so that her breasts were crushed against the hard wall of his chest, her legs tangling with his.

But still it wasn't enough; she needed more. Needed all of him; all of his possession. But the buckle of his belt seemed agonisingly stiff, resisting her attempts to tug it loose, bruising her fingers in frustrating resistance. She was close to tears of exasperation when his hand came over hers, stilling her restless movements.

'Let me…' he muttered, his voice raw with a need that matched her own, his movements every bit as urgent and impatient as hers had been.

But from the moment that she felt the heat of his flesh against her she suddenly wanted to slow everything down. She still felt every bit as hungry as before, more so, if that was possible, but in the instant that she felt the warm velvet-over-steel sensation of his erection nudging at her thighs she was suddenly painfully aware of the fact that it would never be this way again. Not the first time they had come together, but…

The first time they had *made love*.

It hit her like a blow in the face, making her gasp out loud. And as soon as the thought entered her head she knew that she should have realised it in the moment when she had gone to pieces at the sight of Santos's car at the side of the road, almost crushed under the brutal weight of the fallen tree. In that moment when she had been unable to bear the thought of his beautiful body, of Santos himself hurt or injured in any way. So much so that it had almost destroyed her even to imagine it.

And that was because she had fallen in love with him. She was in so deep that just imagining him hurt was worse than actually being injured herself.

She was in love and she was about to make love to the man who had had such an impact on her; the man to whom she'd given her heart, even if he didn't know it. And it was because he didn't know it—would probably never, ever know it—that she hesitated now.

He would never want to know how she felt. Why should he when he didn't believe in love for himself or for anyone else in the world? He didn't believe in love and so he would never want what she most wanted to give him and he could never give her the thing she most needed from him—his love in return.

But even as the thought crossed her mind, she knew that she didn't care.

He couldn't give her that but he could give her this, the passion of his body. And that was all he would give her. So she wanted to take her time with this, savour it, enjoy every moment and store it away in her memory so that one day, when memories were all she had…

'Alexa?'

Santos had notice her withdrawal, the way she had disappeared into her own thoughts, and he raised his dark head, silvery eyes searching her hazel ones, looking deep into her face, into her heart, she could almost believe, feeling that he could see what was buried there.

'What is it? Are you having second thoughts?'

'Oh, no…'

No, no, no! Never that. But she saw the frown that drew

his black brows together and knew that she had to say something to explain her momentary hesitation.

'It's just…do you have anything—any protection?'

She'd managed to distract him and he nodded in agreement. '*Desde luego*—of course…'

Reaching over the side of the bed, he grabbed at his jacket, pulled a leather wallet from the pocket and extracted the necessary small foil packet that was tucked inside.

'So sensible, *belleza*…' he muttered, pressing a warm kiss on her forehead, then one onto each eyelid, pressing them closed. 'So cautious.'

If only he knew that cautious was the last thing she wanted to be. That what she really wanted was to throw all caution to the wind as she had done once before, and give herself to him totally and unreservedly, without the need for any protection—without anything coming between her and the full knowledge of his lovemaking.

But of course for Santos it wasn't *lovemaking*. For him it was just sex, purely physical passion and nothing more. He would always want to be careful, because he wouldn't want any possible consequences from what, for him, was just a passing indulgence in sensual pleasure. The simple fact that he carried condoms with him, so readily available, was potent evidence of that.

As she heard the foil packet tear and knew that he was sheathing himself—to protect her as well as him, she told herself fiercely—she was grateful for the fact that he had closed her eyes with his mouth. In the concealing darkness she could hide for a moment, knowing that her disappointment wouldn't be revealed to him when he looked into her face. Behind her closed lids she could swallow down the weak, revealing tears, draw a much needed breath and bring herself back to calm acceptance of what had to be.

No, not calm. There was nothing calm about the way she

felt. She was hungry, needy, *yearning* both physically and mentally. There was nothing she could do about the mental ache, the one that centred in her heart and spread outwards into every part of her. But she could appease the physical hunger, she could give herself to Santos and know his physical possession, if nothing more. And if that was the only form of love that he would ever believe in, it would have to be enough. She could do that for him, and by doing so she could be almost happy.

And so she reached for him. Closed her hands around his muscled arms and drew him close. Pressed her lips against his and kissed him with all the intensity of the feeling she knew. She opened her mouth to him and let her tongue tangle with his and when he moved over her, parting her legs with one powerful, hair-roughened thigh, she opened herself to him too with a new kind of joy that made her whole body sing in more than the sexual passion that glowed in her veins.

But when at last he entered her, easing into her waiting body in one long, slow, controlled thrust, she felt the need and hunger ignite all over again. Her nerves burned with it, her head spun, her senses were on overload with the feel and scent of him all around her, inside her. Her mouth was on his skin, her fingers clenching over the tight, bunching muscles of his back as she met each strong movement, arching against him to take him more fully into her.

'I needed this,' Santos muttered against her mouth. 'Needed you…'

There was no doubting the truth of his words, it was there in the rush of colour along the carved cheekbones, the febrile glitter that turned his eyes to molten silver. It was in his voice too, in the rough, husky tones that deepened his accent, made it raw and thick in a way that was far removed from his usual clear speech.

'And now you have me,' Alexa returned, kissing the words

onto his lips. Knowing that this was as close as she dared come to the declaration of the way she truly felt. 'All of me—every last little bit…'

The words broke on a gasp of delight as a wickedly knowing move of his strong body broke all trace of her control, taking her to the brink of ecstasy and holding her there. Oblivious to anything and everything beyond him, she could only cling on to his strength, lost, blind, abandoned, her whole being concentrated on the wild sensations she was experiencing, the forceful build-up, the yearning for release…

And then he thrust again and again, taking her right over the edge this time, throwing her into the sensual free-fall of total oblivion while all her senses spun and the world whirled and shattered all around her. A moment later she was crushed tight in his arms, his powerful muscles clenching, his heart pounding underneath her cheek, and she heard his own raw cry as he followed her into the shimmering void, losing himself completely in her body's welcoming embrace.

CHAPTER ELEVEN

THE LIGHT OF the dawn breaking beyond the uncurtained window was what slowly dragged Alexa back to wakefulness from the depths of the deep, exhausted sleep she had fallen into at some late point in the night. Her eyes opened slowly, blinked dreamily, staring up at the white-painted ceiling above her as she struggled to recognise where she was.

In her home, in her bedroom—of course that was where she was. Every instinct told her she was in the all too familiar surroundings, every part of her recognised the wallpaper, the feel of the bed, the plain white bed linen...but at the same time everything seemed and felt so very different that it was as if she had awakened somewhere totally new and strange. Somewhere that she didn't recognise at all.

But then she blinked again, stretching slightly, and her right arm and leg came into contact with the hard warmth of a strong body lying relaxed and totally at ease just beside her. A long, muscled, relaxed *male* body, she acknowledged and with the realisation came the rush of remembrance that told her it was not the room that was new, not her surroundings that were different, but that she herself had changed. The events of the night, and her realisation of the way that she felt about Santos, meant that she would never, ever be the same again.

'Santos...'

She tested his name on her tongue, almost as if trying it on for size, tasting it where she could still sense the essence of him in her mouth. For the moment she didn't need to turn to see the man she loved where he lay relaxed in sleep beside her; her mind was still so full of the images of the night that she needed time to absorb them before she could take the reality of his presence without total overload.

And so she lay there for a time, staring up at the ceiling, reviewing the hours she had spent locked in burning passion. She had lost count of how many times Santos had reached for her, or she for him. Lost track of how often they had come together, experienced the mindless bliss of total orgasm, and then collapsed, exhausted, into sleep. She only knew that the night had passed in a blur of sensual and emotional delights, and that now she faced the prospect of the day ahead with a smile and a glow of anticipation.

Of course, there was no dodging away from the one flaw in her pleasure; no way of avoiding the harsh and bitter truth that Santos had never, and would never say that he loved her. The blazing passion that he had showed her through the night was the only expression of feeling he had ever allowed himself and it was all that he ever would let escape him. And she would be a total fool to ask for more.

But he *had* said that he wanted—needed her. And he had made plain just how much that was true by the force of his desire, the hunger he had shown for her body. And for now that would be enough. It had to be. It was all she was going to get.

The smile that the memory of that desire had brought to her face still lingered as she turned slowly and indolently over in the warmth of the bed, luxuriating in the comfort, the relaxation, even the faint ache of muscles and parts of her body that had received so much attention during the night. And would soon receive that same attention all over again. All she had to do was to rouse Santos from his sleep and…

'*Santos!*'

The smile faded from her lips, his name escaping on a cry of shock and horror, and she came fully wide awake in a rush as she took in the sight before her.

Santos was lying on his stomach, with his face buried in the pillow, the burnished jet of his hair in stark contrast to the crisp white cotton of the covers. The quilt had fallen down to lie across his narrow waist, leaving his long, muscular back exposed. And what brought the sound of shock and horror to Alexa's lips was the sight of several ugly scars that marred the surface of the beautiful olive skin. There was one high up on his right shoulder, another two lower down, close to his spine. All three were just about identical, almost perfectly circular and slightly indented into the skin. Alexa winced at the ugliness of them, the fact that they were clearly old and had not been made recently doing nothing to reduce her distress at the sight.

'*Santos!*' she said again, reaching out an uncertain hand to touch him softly.

She knew that he was awake and that he'd heard her because of a faint twitch of his dark head, and the way his back tensed under her fingertips, every muscle drawing suddenly tight. But he didn't look up, didn't turn towards her.

'What happened?'

For a long couple of seconds she thought that he wasn't going to answer and her heart slammed against her ribcage as she waited tensely for his reaction. But then at last he let out his breath in a long, deep sigh and pushed himself suddenly upright, twisting round so that he was sitting with his back against the bed head, the ugly scars hidden from view.

'If you don't want…' Alexa began, suddenly afraid that she had intruded where he didn't want her to be, crossing over some invisible line that she hadn't even been aware had been drawn between her and the part of his life that he wanted to keep private.

'No…'

With one hand he waved away her concern, but his eyes remained fixed straight ahead of him, staring unfocused at some spot on the far wall.

'It's OK. It happened long ago. Almost thirty years.'

'Thirty…you were a child?'

Santos nodded slowly, still not looking at her. She was sure that he wasn't actually looking at anything but staring into the distance, seeing only his memories.

And whatever those memories were, the tension in his face, the frown that drew the black brows together declared only too clearly that they were far from happy ones.

'You remember that I told you my mother didn't know who my father was?'

Silently Alexa nodded, afraid to speak, afraid she would distract him.

She gave birth to me, that is all, he had said. *I doubt if mi madre even knew who my father was. He could have been any one of a dozen possible candidates.*

'She had no way of knowing which of the men she had been with in the right month or so actually was my father. But she wanted to be on her way, wanted to leave for the new life she was sure was going to be hers in Argentina, with her current man—another new man. Someone who did not want a child, particularly not one fathered by someone else. So *mi madre* left me with *mi padre.*'

'But you said she didn't know…' It burst from Alexa before she realised just what he had said, what the appallingly cynical emphasis he had given the words *mi padre* implied.

'She didn't *know,*' he said now, bringing his knees up under the covers and resting his elbows on them, his face cupped in his hands. 'She just chose one at random—anyone—the closest one to hand. She left me on his doorstep with a note.'

'She left you…'

In spite of the warmth of the room, the soft comfort of the downy quilt, Alexa felt shiveringly cold, her blood suddenly ice in her veins. She tried to imagine a small boy, lost, lonely, abandoned, sitting on a doorstep, waiting for the man who might be his father to open the door. Watching his mother walk away from him. All at once she felt she could begin to understand just why he had declared so obdurately that he didn't believe in love.

'How could she do it?'

'I'm sure she saw it as the perfect solution.'

Bleak and unemotional, the blank statement slashed at Alexa in a way that any more savage declaration could never do. Santos's total lack of feeling somehow, his apparent detachment, made everything so much worse than if he had shouted or sworn.

'It was too bad that the poor bastard she left me with did not feel the same.'

Flinging back the bedclothes, Santos swung his long legs out of the bed, getting to his feet. As he paced across the room, Alexa couldn't help but stare at the beautiful, lean, strong shape of his body, the powerful legs, tight buttocks, the long, sleek line of his back. Last night she had caressed that body, her hands had clung to his shoulders, fingers digging into his back in the throes of ecstasy.

Last night she hadn't known those scars were there.

Today she could not look away from them.

'What happened?'

Her voice croaked embarrassingly. She didn't really want to know, but she knew that she had to find out. Having come this far, there was no turning back.

'What happened?'

He actually sounded as if he was considering the question. As if he was trying to remember what had happened because it was buried in the mists of time. Alexa had no doubt at all that the truth was the exact opposite. That he remembered far, far too well. And because of that, his pretence at hesitation made the sensation of something vile and slimy sliding over her skin.

'Santos—don't,' she tried but he wasn't listening.

'He kept me—for a while. He thought I might be useful around the house.'

'What could you do? You were what—three?'

'Just. But he did not know much about kids. He thought I would be better at the jobs he wanted done than I was. He hated it when I was slow or clumsy. He hated it especially when he'd been drinking. When he had been drinking then he was impatient—and mean.'

'Santos, what did he do?'

Santos swung round to face her so that she could no longer see the scars on his back. But she still knew they were there. And even if she had tried to forget them then the hard, tight set of his face would have been a painful reminder whenever she looked at him.

'When he drank, he also smoked heavily. If I got in the way—or was slow…'

He didn't finish the sentence. He didn't need to. Alexa knew that her face must have revealed how much she understood. How she knew exactly what he was trying to say. And how she wished that she didn't.

Oh, no, no, no, no!

In her mind's eye she was seeing again those scars, the round shape of them, and at the same time her horrified imagination was showing a smoking, glowing cigarette tip.

'Oh, dear God!'

'And the other scar—the one on your hand…?' She couldn't finish the question.

'Yes,' was all Santos said. It was all he needed to say. There was no way she wanted him to expand on the simple syllable.

It was no wonder he didn't believe in love. No wonder he

trusted no one, believed in no one. How could he believe in something that he had never learned? Something that no one had ever shown him existed? After a betrayal—betrayals—like that, he must believe that he was unlovable himself, that no one would ever love him.

Her mind went back to Santos's declaration that she should marry him—there was no way that she could call it a proposal. Of course he couldn't couch that in terms of love, she saw that now.

'What did you do?'

'I ran away as soon as I could. I ended up in a children's home.'

'And didn't you tell anyone?'

'What would have been the point? It was in the past—I'd got away.'

Santos was moving around the room, collecting up his clothes, restoring order. She couldn't help wondering if he was doing the same in his mind as well.

'And later I'd heard that he'd died—an overdose. There was nothing to be gained from going back over it. I moved on.'

He'd moved on, but he'd taken the scars with him. Scars on his mind as well as on his body. And although he said he'd put it behind him, it was still there. Still darkening his life, still making it impossible for him to build a loving relationship. But he had opened up to her. He had told her the terrible story of his childhood. Was she a fool to read something into that?

'I'd like to take a shower.' Santos's voice, all practicality and matter-of-fact tone, intruded into her thoughts.

While she had been absorbed in thinking over what he had been saying, interpreting it, finding possible repercussions that might result from it, he had been getting his life back under control. His clothes—and hers—were off the floor and on the bed, and now he wanted a shower. His day was going to begin, it seemed, with everything as normal and the uncomfortable revelations he had made now tidily put away.

'Of course…'

The way she had been feeling when she had woken this morning she would have suggested that she join him, that they make the shower a way of continuing the sensual pleasure of the night. But there was no way she dared do that now. The mood was gone, every last trace of sensuality between them evaporated as if it had never been. Santos didn't even have a smile for her now. In fact, he never so much as glanced at her as he snatched up his clothes and headed for the bathroom. A few moments later she heard the sound of the shower water pounding down and it was impossible not to wonder if he was determined to wash the scent of her from his body, sluice away all traces of the night they had shared and so erase it from his memory as well.

And yet he had opened up to her…

Why the hell had he opened up to her?

Santos stood under the shower, the force turned up to the highest it would go, and let the water pound down onto his skull as he went back over what had just happened. Alexa had seen the scars and, inevitably, had asked about them. It had happened before. Other women had seen the marks on his back and some had asked about them.

But he had never answered anyone truthfully before.

Every other time he had fobbed them off with some vague murmur about an accident. Nothing precise; nothing revealing. And they had been satisfied with that. As he had been satisfied with not revealing too much about himself.

But this time it had not been like that. This time he had had to tell the whole damn story. The one he had never let anyone in on before. Alexa would not have let him fob her off; he knew that. And he had shocked her to hell. He'd seen it in her eyes, in the way that that mossy hazel gaze had widened, darkened in horror. He'd shocked himself too with the realisation of how much he had wanted to tell her, how much he had wanted her to know about him.

And he had never felt more exposed in his life.

Being naked in a woman's bedroom wasn't a new experience. He had had his share of lovers over the years, but this was the first time that he had actually *felt* naked. And it wasn't a feeling he liked.

In fact if the truth was told, he had been feeling this way from the moment he had met Alexa at the party before the wedding. She hadn't been at all what he had been expecting, and one look at her had rocked his sense of reality, the way he had felt about life.

If only she had been the daughter he was going to marry. The thought had shot through his head even as he had held out his hand in greeting and felt it taken in hers. If she had been the sister he was to marry then the whole marriage deal would have been a very different prospect. But he was committed, the wedding was planned, and so he had forced himself to hold back, to give nothing away.

And now Alexa *was* the sister whose hand in marriage was offered as part of the deal. Her bastard of a father had quite happily agreed to his other daughter being a replacement for the one who had run out on him on the wedding day. Anything to save his own cowardly skin. And if Alexa truly was as innocent as he suspected then learning that would have been almost as devastating for her as the way that his own parent had walked out on him.

He pushed his head back under the shower, lifting his face up to the force of the water and slicking back his hair with hard fingers that dug into his skull as he tried to close off his mind to the unsettled, restless thoughts that plagued him day and night. There was only one thing he was sure of and that was that he had no intention of letting this Montague daughter run out on him.

This one he was going to make sure of. This one he wanted willing. And after last night he felt sure that willing was exactly what she would be.

The telephone was ringing somewhere downstairs as he opened the bathroom door and he heard Alexa running down the stairs as she went to answer it. Santos followed her down, buttoning up his shirt as he went but leaving it hanging loose over the waistband of his jeans.

'Coffee?' he asked as he passed her in the hall just as she reached the phone. She had pulled on a pale blue cotton robe and was belting it around her waist as she picked up the receiver.

'Mmm...'

Her reply was distracted, her attention on the phone.

'Dad!'

Of course. He'd told her to speak to her father. But, *maldito sea*, he thought she'd done that last night. She'd been on the phone when he'd come back to the house. He'd really believed that everything was out in the open then. Now it seemed that that assumption might have been completely wrong.

Alexa had known that it had to be her father on the phone as soon as she'd heard it ringing. She'd asked him to ring her back as soon as he got her message and this was obviously him doing just that.

Talk to your father, Santos had said. And she'd planned to do that, determined to do that before she ever saw him again. But last night fate had intervened—she hadn't been able to get through to her father, and Santos had come back to the house so unexpectedly...

So would anything have changed if she'd spoken to her father first? Her heart skipped a beat as she asked herself the question. She had let things run away with her last night. Was she going to have to regret being so impulsive? Had she made a terrible mistake?

How bad could it be?

'Dad, I need to talk to you…'

But her father wasn't listening.

'Have you seen him? Have you seen Santos Cordero? He said he was on his way to you.'

'He's—' Alexa began but her father cut right across her, wanting to speak first, determined to make her listen.

So she listened. And with every word that came from her father's mouth she felt more of the blood draining from her face, the strength leaving her legs until she sagged against the wall for support.

How bad could it be? she had asked herself. And the answer to that was it could be the worst. The very worst.

CHAPTER TWELVE

ALEXA HAD NO idea how long her father had been talking before he finally ground to a halt. She only knew that when he did she barely had enough strength or mental ability to say anything in reply. She could only manage something vague and unformed, something along the lines of yes, she understood. Yes, she saw that he had had no possible alternative, not one that would solve the situation, keep her stepmother from a total breakdown and himself out of gaol.

Out of gaol.

There it was. There was the very worst-case scenario summed up right there. She had always known that her father could be totally selfish, the wife he was devoted to even worse—but this!

Because of his own stupid actions—his stupid, *illegal* actions—Stanley Montague had risked not only his home and his income but also his own freedom. If Santos had prosecuted him then he would be in prison right now.

But the prosecution was still only a threat as long as Santos Cordero got what he wanted. And what he wanted was a link to the Montague name through marriage.

He had meant every single word he said when he had announced that her family owed him a wife.

I've come for you.

And all the time she listened to her father explaining and apologising, she knew that Santos was waiting in the kitchen with his coffee and his knowing smile. And his damn hateful, arrogant conviction that he had her right where he wanted her.

Or so he thought.

But he did, didn't he? He had her exactly where he wanted her. Where he'd always wanted her right from the very start. He had her trapped, with nowhere to turn, no way out, no possible answer. Not unless she let everyone down, ruined her whole family, very likely drove her stepmother into a mental breakdown.

And sent her father to gaol for embezzlement.

There, now she'd admitted it to herself. Because that was what her father had admitted to her in the phone call. That he had been stupid, totally, crazily foolish. He'd squandered every last penny the Montague family owned—with a lot of help from her greedy, grasping stepmother, Alexa had no doubt. And then, to make matters worse, he'd 'borrowed' some money from a business deal he had been supposed to be planning, with Santos Cordero as his partner.

Alexa shook her head in despair, raking both hands through the fall of her hair and then rubbing the palms over her aching eyes. Only her father could call embezzling funds that had been meant for a business deal 'borrowing.' Only her father could have then spent that money, sending good money after bad, and so ended up in this terrible position.

And putting her into a far worse one.

She knew that her father's weakness, his selfishness, should hurt her. That his betrayal of her to Santos should wound her terribly. But the truth was that nothing her father said or did could touch her because there wasn't a spot on her heart that Santos hadn't already devastated. And Santos's callousness hurt far more than anything else.

'One Montague bride is as good as any other when this was

only meant to be a dynastic marriage…' The callous words came back to haunt her from the night of the wedding that had never been.

'I've come for you,' he had said. And she had refused to believe that he had meant it. She'd even allowed herself to think, to dream, that he might actually be starting to feel something for her. That he had opened up to her because…

'No!'

Alexa slammed her clenched fist against her mouth to hold back the cry of distress that almost escaped her.

No, there had to be some way out of this. She was not going to let this happen. One thing she was damn sure of was that she was not going down without a fight. Santos might think that he had what he wanted on a plate, but she'd see about that. Somehow.

But first she had to get dressed. There was no way she could face the arrogant, manipulative swine while just wearing the blue robe that clung to her figure rather too tightly, the material so well-worn in places that in a certain light it was practically transparent. And she had nothing at all on underneath.

A fact of which Santos, of course, was only too well aware. Alexa felt a hot tide of embarrassment flood her body at the thought of how easily he had been able to do exactly as he pleased with her. How he had had no problem at all in enticing her into bed. If she was strictly honest with herself, then she had to admit that she had practically done all the work for him. She had flung herself into his arms, into his bed…

OK, into *her* bed, taking him with her. She had given herself to him without a thought. He must have thought that all his birthdays had come at once. And that his ruthless plan for a marriage of convenience had worked so perfectly.

Well, she'd see about that, she told herself as she made her way upstairs to dress. If there was any way out of this she was going to find it. Santos Cordero had to learn that he couldn't just walk in and take over people's lives. Someone had to stand up to him…

But why, oh why did it have to be her?

She wished that she could have a shower, longed to stand under the hottest water and scrub her body hard in the vain hope that she could erase the memory of his touch, the imprint of his caresses and his kisses that she felt she wore like a brand that had been seared into her skin, marking her out as his like some slave girl of long ago who was her master's property for life. But she didn't dare to linger, knowing that if she stayed up here too long then Santos would get curious, and then impatient, and she feared that he would then come upstairs, following her to find out just what she was doing.

He might arrive while she was still dressing and, even if she had the time to pull on her clothes before he arrived, just the thought of being in her bedroom, with the bedcovers still tangled from their passion of the night before, the sheets and pillowcases still holding the imprint of his body, the scent of his skin, was almost more than she could bear.

And she had thought that she loved him!

Her own foolish thoughts came back to haunt her as she made her way back down the stairs. How could she have believed herself in love with a man who manipulated people in this way? Who effectively bought a wife without ever offering her any sort of emotional commitment?

A man who, when marriage to one wife had not materialised, simply turned to the next person on the list of prospective partners?

'I've come for you…' Well, she'd see about that.

Outside the kitchen door, Alexa drew in a deep breath, squaring her shoulders and lifting her head, tilting her chin defiantly before she marched into the room.

And knew immediately that she was only fooling herself

if she tried to deny her feelings for this man. The sudden clenching of her heart at the sight of him where he sat at the small dining table, his black hair still crisply damp from his shower, his blue shirt hanging loose over the waistband of his jeans, his long legs stretched out and his bare feet crossed at the ankles, told its own story. There was no way on earth that she could deny the way she felt about this man. Feelings that at any other time would have led her to accept oh, so willingly the idea of marriage to him.

Feelings that she must fight to suppress, to put right out of her mind if she was to be able to cope with the situation she now found herself in.

'At last,' Santos greeted her casually.

'I wanted to get dressed.' Alexa's tone was stiff with the effort she was making to control it. 'I feel better like this.'

The look he slanted her from those pale eyes, skimming over her appearance in a clean pair of denim jeans and a soft green sweater, questioned her need to get dressed at all so clearly that she could almost guess at exactly what he was thinking. Why put on any clothes when he had every intention of taking them all off again very soon? that expression said, and determinedly Alexa set herself to ignore it. They were not going to be heading for bed at any time in the near future—never again if she had her way. When her weak and traitorous body cried out in protest and her eyes drank in the sight of him, long and lean and whipcord-strong as he lounged at the table, she forced herself back under control with a vicious effort and lifted her chin a touch higher, defying him to put his thoughts into words.

But Santos either didn't notice or decided not to comment if he did.

'Your coffee's over there...'

He waved a hand in the direction of a mug that stood on the nearby worktop.

'I poured it when I heard you on your way back down so it's quite fresh.'

Alexa marched over to the mug, snatched it up and, twisting round, emptied the contents sharply into the sink, watching with a mixture of satisfaction and regret as the brown liquid whirled around the plughole and then disappeared down the drainpipe. She would have loved a nice, reviving mug of coffee—in fact, there was nothing she would have liked better—but she felt that a gesture needed to be made and besides, there was the suspicion that the drink would choke her if she so much as attempted to swallow.

Santos watched her actions with narrowed eyes, just one eyebrow slightly raised to question her response.

'Something wrong with that?' he drawled lazily, but the gaze that he fixed on her face was anything but indolent. Behind those thick black lashes, the pale eyes gleamed so intently that she almost felt the burn of them on her skin.

'This isn't going to work, Santos!' she declared, deciding to jump straight into confrontation rather than dance around the topic for a moment.

'What isn't going to work?'

'This scheme you've come up with to get yourself a wife by blackmail.'

'You've talked to your father.' It was cold and flat and hard.

'Yes, I've talked to my father—that is what you advised yesterday if you recall…'

Just why had he done that? Why had he not come right out and explained the situation, enjoying the power game, as she might have expected? Because she wouldn't have believed him? Or could there be some other possible reason?

'So now I know what you've been up to.'

'What your father has been up to,' Santos corrected, cold and stiff and totally impassive. The atmosphere in the room had iced over as if the temperature had dropped a hundred degrees or more so that she almost expected to see her breath steam in the air as it did outdoors.

'Well, yes, what he did was very wrong, and of course he can't just get away with that. But I know why he did it. He did it for Petra. He always was a fool where she was concerned and he could never refuse her anything. She never understood about the burden of death duties when Grandpa died, and she just went on spending and spending. The money will have to be paid back.'

'You say that so very glibly.' Santos put his own mug down on the table and leaned forward, watching her intently. 'Did your father happen to mention just how much money was involved?'

'It was obviously a lot.'

'You could say that,' Santos drawled and named an amount that had her mouth dropping open in horror as she grabbed at a nearby chair for support. 'You really didn't know?'

'I...'

'Do you really think that I would concern myself with anything less?'

'I...' Alexa tried again but her mind was spinning in shock and dismay. She felt as if the ground she was standing on had suddenly started to crumble beneath her and large cracks were opening up, threatening to send her flying into some dreadful great cavern.

Of course, she should have known—or at least suspected. It was no wonder that her father had been looking ill and grey. The evidence was there in the hysteria that had gripped Petra, the pallor of Stanley's drawn, worried face on the wedding day. And before that it had been in the impossibly extravagant lifestyle her father, stepmother and half-sister had been living over the past couple a years. A lifestyle she hadn't thought to enquire into. But then, deep down, she knew that if she had asked no one would have told her anything. Just as they hadn't told her anything about the circumstances of the wedding. Not until now, when they thought that she could do something to help.

'I'm sorry,' she managed at last. 'I never realised it was as bad as that. But do you really think that any amount of money justifies playing with people's lives? Manipulating them into marrying you whether they want to or not?'

Santos sighed and pushed his hands through his hair, flexing his shoulders as if to ease some intolerable tension there.

'When I said that you should talk to your father, I had thought that you would get confirmation of the truth. I did not manipulate your sister into marrying me. She made it plain that she was attracted to me, and that my wealth was no small part of that attraction. She was the one who suggested marriage.'

If he'd told her this on the day of the wedding, she would have refuted it angrily, Alexa acknowledged. Now she no longer had the luxury of doubting it.

And that forced her to look back at the things that Natalie had said that had pushed her into action.

'I thought I could do this, Lexa,' her sister had said. '*I really wanted to*—but it just isn't going to work now. If John hadn't come into my life I would have gone ahead…but he did…and meeting him has changed everything.'

Natalie had never really told her the full truth. She'd never fully admitted how one part of her loved the prospect of being Santos's bride. The thought of the money and the celebrity, the excitement of being in all the lifestyle magazines. But meeting the man she really cared for had brought her up short, making her realize she needed so much more—emotionally— if she was going to commit herself to marriage.

'She knew that I wanted heirs to my fortune, and that being linked with the Montague name would open doors in society where money would not. And she wanted the lifestyle she'd always had. So she suggested a plan that would be of mutual benefit.'

And not believing in love—believing himself to be *unlovable*—Santos had found in that proposition the answer to everything he wanted.

'I would have been good to her, Alexa. She would never have wanted for anything. And of course, if she was my wife, then I could hardly prosecute my father-in-law. But I would have him where I could see him and I'd be able to keep a very close eye on anything he and his wife got up to.'

'Not prosecuting him—that wasn't part of the bargain?'

She read the answer in his face, but he obviously needed to confirm it.

'I don't even know how much Natalie was aware of her father's position. She knew he had money troubles, but I doubt if she knew just how they'd come about.'

'But in the end that wasn't enough for her. Not when she met John.'

'No, she surprised me there,' Santos admitted thoughtfully. 'This new man must be something special.'

Just for a moment Alexa wondered if he might actually take that thought a little further, if he would use the word 'love' as the one thing her sister had wanted more than money. But when Santos spoke again she knew a terrible sense of disappointment.

'But it left me with a problem. Your father still owed me the money.'

'And so you decided, quite cold-bloodedly, that I could replace my sister. No?' she questioned when he shook his head slowly.

'No, Alexa. Never that. Can't you see that there is never anything I do where you are concerned that is *cold*-blooded? The truth is the exact opposite. You heat my blood until I can't think straight. You make me do crazy things.'

Now Alexa really needed the chair she was holding on to. Her legs had turned to cotton wool beneath her and she had to sit down before she fell down. But as she sank into the seat opposite him Santos pushed his chair back with a rough, scraping sound and got to his feet, swinging away to pace restlessly around the kitchen. And that felt far worse than before because, sitting down, she was so much more aware of how big and dark and dangerously imposing he was.

'Wh-what sort of things?'

'Things I would never have imagined were possible. Things like coming here to return a pair of shoes that I hated the sight of because they reminded me of how badly they had damaged your feet.'

'You said you had come for me.' Her voice shook with the combination of laughter and tears that that last sentence had created.

'And I had. I couldn't get you out of my mind. I wanted you so badly that I couldn't stay away. And I knew that you wanted me too. Of course, it also solved the problem of your father...'

'Of course,'

Alexa's voice was low, shaken. But then what else had she expected?

Had she really thought that there would be a wild declaration of love after all this? That Santos would suddenly find that most vital emotion had been locked away in his heart all that time? He didn't believe in love, didn't even know what it was, so how could he feel it? He wanted her, that was all. It might be enough for him. But it wasn't enough for her.

She loved this man desperately. But could she love enough for the two of them? She didn't think so.

She might love him now but without being loved back, without anything to feed it then would that love be strong enough to survive? Could she love this man for the rest of her life and know that he did not love her without it destroying her, leaving her empty and broken because she was getting nothing in return?

Nothing but the burning passion which was all he felt now. And which one day, inevitably, must surely burn itself out.

'And so you came here to demand that I marry you.'

'Not demand. It was what you wanted too.'

'No.'

She forced herself to say it and knew from the way that he suddenly stopped pacing, the way he spun on his heel, whirling round to face her, that she had shocked him almost as much as she had shocked herself by flinging the single syllable out into the room, splintering the atmosphere with its force.

'No,' she managed again but with less strength this time. Deep inside she could feel the way that the tension in the atmosphere had started to reach her chest. It was constricting her lungs, making it almost impossible to breathe, and there was a terrible sensation as if some hard, cruel hand had reached in to take hold of her heart, crushing and twisting it brutally, threatening to rip it right in two.

She had to say this because it was the only way she could survive in the long run, but saying it right here and now was almost more than she could bear. It was destroying her, smashing her self and her love into tiny little pieces, and yet she had no alternative but to do it.

'No?'

If she had reached out and slapped him right in the face then Santos could not have sounded more stunned, more shocked. His pale eyes were so clouded that the soft grey was almost opaque and she could read nothing of his thoughts in them.

With a huge effort of will Alexa forced herself to her feet, making herself face him, look into those shuttered eyes, though the expression in them made her tremble all over, her mouth drying painfully over the words she needed to force out.

'No, I don't want to marry you.'

'Liar.' It was low and soft but deadly, like a striking snake. 'You don't mean that.'

'Oh, but I do.' Somehow she found the strength to say it.

'I don't want to marry you, not when it is just a way of paying my father's debts, saving him from being prosecuted…'

'All right!'

Santos flung up his hands in a gesture that almost looked like defeat.

'All right—let's take your father out of this. Let this just be between you and me.'

If her head had been spinning before, now she felt as if it might actually explode from the pressure of trying to contain the number of wild, whirling and totally contradictory thoughts within it. He couldn't mean what he seemed to be saying—he just couldn't.

'I don't understand—what do you mean?'

'We will forget about your father—'

'I can't! What he did was wrong. I've accused you of using people—but he can be just as bad. I know that he told you where to find me.'

Those silvery eyes were strangely gentle as if he understood just what she was going through—which, of course, he did.

'That was his poisonous wife. He only stood back and let her do it.'

Putting his palms and fingers together as people did when they were praying, Santos used both his hands to emphasise his words as he spoke.

'I will forget about the money your father stole from me. I'll write off his debts—forget the idea of prosecution—clear the whole thing. I'll find it far harder to accept that he was prepared to use you to save his own skin. I doubt if I will ever forgive him for that. But if you ask me to then I will—if you'll marry me.'

Accept it! Alexa's heart screamed, desperate to agree. Accept it, you fool; it's as much as you're going to get. Accept it and don't ask for more. You can be happy with this.

Happy for now.

She'd actually opened her mouth to agree, had formed the word 'yes' on her tongue when bitter truth hit home once again, forcing her to adjust what she had been about to say.

'And why do you want to marry me?'

'Because I *want* you, damn it!'

Striding swiftly across the room, he caught hold of her hands, held them tightly, both her fists surrounded by his broad palms, his long fingers. His touch was warm and strong and it should have felt comforting, balm to her wounded heart. But the truth was that it felt exactly the opposite, twisting the brutal knife even deeper into her desolated soul.

'I want you so much that I feel I'll go mad without you in my life, in my bed. Didn't last night tell you that?'

'Last night...' Alexa began, then broke off, unable to complete the sentence.

Last night I thought you cared, she wanted to say. Last night I thought that when you called me *querida* you meant it. If last night had been just the beginning then I might have been able to accept it, to think that there was so much more to look forward to, that one day you might come to love me.

But that had been before she had woken up today and seen those scars on his back. Before she had realised how deep the scars on his mind, on his heart had gone. How they had killed every hope there had ever been that Santos could feel love. And today, with every word that he had said he had only dug the grave of those hopes deeper and deeper.

He had wanted her. He still wanted her. But wanting was not love.

It wasn't enough. Not when she needed so much more from him.

CHAPTER THIRTEEN

'DON'T TELL ME that you didn't enjoy last night,' Santos said now, his voice rough and raw, his searing gaze burning into her. 'Don't tell me that it wasn't what you wanted—what you still want. Let me—'

No, Alexa wanted to cry, seeing what was in his eyes, knowing what he intended and wanting desperately to avoid it. But the word was never spoken aloud, pushed back into her throat by the rapid descent of his mouth, the fierce pressure that forced her lips open under his, crushing them in the force of his passion.

And for a moment she yielded. For the space of several frantic heartbeats she could do nothing else. She wanted his kiss, wanted it desperately and although it tore at her wounded heart she couldn't hold back her response, couldn't stop herself from putting all her love and her hunger into kissing him back. Feeling it, Santos caught her up in his arms, crushing her closer, taking her mouth with the force of the primitive male passion that had him totally in its grip. And just for a moment or two Alexa let herself enjoy the bitter-sweet delight that it brought her.

But only for a moment or two. The second it went on longer than that the bitter-sweet tipped over into agony, into something she couldn't bear any longer, not knowing that it was all she could feel. And so, summoning up all the strength she possessed, and some she had no idea she could be capable of, she pressed her hands up against the wall of his chest and pushed as hard as she could, wrenching her mouth away from his with a force that drove her halfway across the room, panting with distress and unable to look him in the face for fear of the cold flames of anger that she knew must burn in his eyes.

'No!' she managed at last, her voice cracking desperately under the force of her despair. 'Last night was—was fun. I enjoyed it, yes. But that's not all there is to marriage.'

'It was more than fun.'

Santos too was breathing hard, each breath seeming to rasp rawly in his chest, and his eyes seemed totally colourless, almost translucent above cheeks that had lost all colour in the intensity of his response.

'It's what I want from marriage. And I want more of it.'

And so did she, Alexa admitted to herself. So why was she holding out like this? Why should she deny herself this, at least, when it was what she wanted so much?

'I want more of it too,' she admitted and watched his head go back sharply in disbelief, seeing something that flashed in his eyes that startled and stunned her.

It amazed her so much that she suddenly had the courage to take a huge chance; to risk everything she had on one enormous gamble. What did she have to lose anyway? There was nothing more that could be taken away from her. It was all or nothing anyway.

'I'm prepared to share your bed—in fact I'll enjoy that— but I will not marry you.'

All or nothing. But she knew that she had gambled and lost when she saw how Santos's expression changed, his face closing up in rejection of what she had said.

'It's marriage or nothing,' he flung at her, a cold, hard verbal challenge.

'Why are you so insistent on marriage?'

And why did she have to keep asking? Why did she keep laying herself open to the pain she knew that he could inflict with just a word, just a look?

'You know why. I want children—heirs. And I want you.'

At least he'd spared her the added misery of reminding her that the status the Montague name brought was important to him too. Not that it could make her feel any worse. She had never believed that a heart could break. But she felt now that she knew that it could, cracking into many pieces inside her chest.

He saw something in the look that she gave him, something she couldn't conceal, no matter how hard she tried.

'What else do you want?' he demanded harshly. 'Don't ask for something I can't give you.'

'Marriage or nothing?' she said softly, sadly, knowing there was no other answer. At least the pain was so bad that it actually stopped the tears at the backs of her eyes. There was no way she could have endured to let them fall. 'Then I'm afraid that it has to be nothing.'

If he had argued, she knew she would have gone to pieces. She could fight herself or she could fight him, but she couldn't contend with them both at once.

But Santos didn't even try to persuade her into any other frame of mind. Instead with one long, searching look into her face, he turned and went silently out of the room. Standing frozen in misery in the middle of the kitchen, she heard him heading upstairs to fetch his shoes, then come down a few moments later. Far too few moments later, Alexa acknowledged as she watched him grab his coat from the hook in the hall and pull it on before without another word he headed for the door.

Look back at me—just once, Alexa begged him in the privacy of her own thoughts, then immediately contradicted herself, pleading with him *not* to turn round, knowing it was more than she could bear if she saw his beloved face one more time and saw stamped on it the determination to leave her, never to have loved her.

'*Adios.*' Santos flung the single word over his shoulder as he turned the key in the lock, wrenched open the door. And then, just in case she hadn't understood, 'Goodbye, Alexa.'

Goodbye. She let the word form silently on her lips but couldn't bring herself to say it. Goodbye, my love.

Tears were blurring her eyes and she blinked them fiercely away, needing to be able to see him clearly this one last time. She watched his tall, straight back stiffen, saw him square his shoulders as he prepared to step out into the morning air, cold and still after the wild storms of the night before.

And stared in disbelief as he hesitated, stopped.

'*No lo puedo,*' he said. 'I cannot…'

'You…'

For several long, fraught moments Alexa struggled to find the strength to say anything. She couldn't see Santos's face and so she had no idea what thoughts were going through his mind.

'You can't—what?'

Slowly he turned to her once again and she could barely recognise his face, the skin was drawn so tightly across his cheekbones, and his eyes were dark with shadows that he didn't try to hide from her.

'Don't ask me to leave. I cannot do it.'

Twice Alexa tried to form the question. Twice her voice broke, failed her, and she had to swallow hard to relieve the tension in her throat. But Santos waited, seeming to understand intuitively just how important this was.

'Why can't you do it?' she managed at last.

'I can't leave you.' It was as simple and as straightforward as that.

'Santos…' Alexa began but he lifted up a hand to silence her, his burning eyes intent on her face.

'No—let me. I'll give you answers. I don't know if they

are the answers you want but they're the only ones that I have. Please listen and then…'

He broke off as if unable to say—or to face—what would happen 'and then…'

And it was the simple fact of the way that Santos, normally the one so totally in control, so totally sure of what he wanted to say, so sure of what should be said, was unable to finish the sentence, was hesitating over what to say next, that kept her frozen, silent, waiting until he could find the words that were needed.

She didn't know where this was heading. She only knew that Santos had been about to leave and then he had turned back. But he still stood between her and the door, with it hanging wide open behind him. All he had to do was to turn in that direction again, and walk, and she knew she would have lost him. For good.

But for now he was here. And she needed to listen to him.

'Tell me.' She spoke softly, knowing there was nothing else she could say.

Santos nodded slowly, drew in a deep, uneven breath.

'Just over a week ago, I had my life all planned out. I was supposed to be getting married to a woman who would bring me everything I wanted—everything I thought I needed. It was all carefully rationalised, totally under my control…'

And control was what he had needed. The adult male was determined to enforce the control that the little boy who had been abandoned, who had been abused, had never had over his fate.

'And I knew that it would work. Natalie and I were a well-planned business deal. But I would have treated her well. She would have wanted for nothing. But then…'

He hesitated, raked both hands through his hair, his eyes looking clouded and distant as if he was focusing on something a long way away, something he could barely see.

'Then at the party before the wedding I met someone else. My bride-to-be's sister…'

At Alexa's sudden gasp of surprise those silvery eyes came up to hers in a swift, flashing look, one that focused intently on her face—and stayed there, watching every flicker of emotion that crossed her features, every tiny change of expression.

'You unsettled me,' he said, the words breaking on a short, self-deprecatory laugh. 'You did more than that. I couldn't take my eyes off you.'

'Then?' Alexa breathed in shock.

'Then,' Santos confirmed, 'I'd been told that Natalie was the beauty but you were the dowdy, bookish one, the spinster librarian. I didn't see any dowdy spinster. I saw someone who intrigued me, someone who caught my eye and held it. Someone...'

He sighed again, shaking his head once more as he recalled those thoughts.

'Someone I needed to put out of my mind if I was to go ahead with my plans. Those carefully thought-out, business-like plans. If I gave in to the attraction I felt to you, if I lost control, then everything would be ruined. But then on my wedding day, things didn't turn out in any way as they were planned. And at the end of the day that should have seen me married, my planning fulfilled, the contracts signed, instead I was in a position where not one but two Montague girls had walked out on me.'

'I'm sorry...' Alexa put in but the words faded into nothing as she saw the way he was looking at her. The unexpected light in his eyes.

'Two of you walked away but there was only one of you I gave a damn about. Only one of you that I couldn't get out of my mind. When you told me that Natalie wasn't coming to the wedding, that she'd jilted me, I was furious, my pride was hurt, but I was determined not to show it.'

'The reception.'

'The reception.' Santos nodded. 'Everything was going to

go ahead as planned. No one was going to see me show any reaction—least of all the family of the woman I was supposed to have married. And I had another plan up my sleeve.'

'Me?'

'You,' he confirmed. 'I thought you were in on everything right from the start. That you had known about your father.'

'I didn't! I swear…' Alexa began but Santos held up a hand to silence her.

'I know that now, but I wasn't thinking straight right then. I was angry—I wanted someone to pay for what had happened. And I thought that person would be you. But then you walked out on me too and suddenly everything changed. Where Natalie's defection left me with hurt pride, an outraged sense of being used…when you left, I missed *you*. I couldn't stop thinking about you; I wanted you back. I would have done anything to get you back. Including turning up here to demand that you took your sister's place.'

'Bringing with you the most uncomfortable pair of shoes I've ever worn.' Alexa's laughter was weak but it was there, and he heard it and his face changed suddenly.

'Those shoes were tearing your poor feet to ribbons. I cannot understand how you could even stand up in them.'

And he *cared*. It was written all over his face. It was there in the burn of his eyes, the shake in his voice. She was beginning to be able to read him, this man who didn't believe in love.

'I missed you, Alexa. I wanted you. I couldn't go on without you. But I didn't know what was happening to me. I didn't understand how I felt. I didn't know what it was.'

Of course not, Alexa thought, her heart aching for his confusion. He didn't know what love was so how could he recognise it?

'When I said I didn't believe in love, I meant that I didn't know how to do it—how to love, I mean. I didn't think it existed, so I didn't even know what it was I was feeling. No one had ever made me feel that way before. I thought it was just wanting—wanting you more than any other woman I'd ever met. And that was bad enough. But then…'

'Then?' Alexa prompted again when he broke off and rubbed both his hands across his face in a gesture of tiredness and confusion that caught on her heart and tugged hard. 'Then what?'

'Then you asked about the scars on my back—and I talked about my mother. For the first time in my life I talked to someone about my mother.'

Alexa's breath caught in her throat. Her head was spinning with the importance of that last sentence. Did he know what he was saying? Did he know the huge compliment he was paying her?

It seemed he did because apparently without being aware of it he had taken a single step—then another—towards her.

Away from the door.

'And when I tried to leave just now—when you said you wouldn't marry me—I couldn't. I couldn't walk away from you because I realised that what I had felt when you walked away from me that day of the wedding wasn't new. It was something I'd felt just once before—when my mother walked away from me. And I knew then why you wouldn't marry me.'

Alexa drew in her breath on a long, ragged sigh and started to speak even as she let it out again.

'Let me tell you why—' she began but broke off as she realised that Santos had moved even closer, that he was reaching out for her hand, taking it in his.

'No—let me tell you,' he said sombrely. 'Because now I think I understand. You wouldn't marry me because I said marriage or nothing. And I was offering nothing—nothing that you wanted. I wanted marriage because I wanted to have you—hold you—I wanted to keep you with me, make sure that you never walked away from me again. In that I was as bad as my mother—your father. I thought I could control you, make you do what I wanted. But what I should have been offering you was the one thing that would have kept you with me for ever if you'd wanted it.'

He paused, looking deep into her eyes, and Alexa felt as if her legs had turned to water at the sight of the powerful emotion she saw burning there. But still she needed him to say it.

He didn't disappoint her.

'You wanted my love.'

'Oh Santos…'

'But I didn't recognise what I was feeling, so how could I say the word? Until I realised that if I didn't say it, then I had to leave. And I couldn't leave…Alexa—what I've said—'

'Sounds a lot like love to me,' Alexa managed, her voice catching, breaking on the words. 'And I should know because that's what I've been feeling too.'

'It is?'

The change in his face was stunning. The light that glowed in his eyes warmed her right through to her soul and his grip on her hands tightened, drawing her close to him until she was hard up against the warm strength of his body and it was the only place in the world that she wanted to be.

'You love me?'

'I love you,' Alexa assured him. 'I love you with all my heart—with everything that's in me. Without your love I couldn't face a future with you, but with it you are all the future I will ever need.'

'And you'll marry me? You'll marry me and be my lover? And now that I know what I'm feeling is love—will you let me love you for the rest of your life?'

'I can't think of anything I'd want more. Yes, Santos, I'll marry you—and together we'll learn about how wonderful love can be when it's shared. When two become one.'

She sighed her happiness as Santos's arms came round her

and she lifted her face for his kiss. A long, deep, giving, *loving* kiss such as she'd never known in her life before.

Behind him the door slammed closed, shutting out the rest of the world and leaving them in their own private, special place where the only thing that they needed was each other and the love they had built between them.

* * * * *

*Harlequin is 60 years old,
and Harlequin Blaze is celebrating!
After all, a lot can happen in 60 years,
or 60 minutes...or 60 seconds!
Find out what's going down in Blaze's
heart-stopping new mini-series,*
FROM 0 TO 60!
*Getting from "Hello" to "How was it?"
can happen fast....*

Here's a sneak peek of the first book,
A LONG, HARD RIDE
*by Alison Kent
Available March 2009*

"Is that for me?" Trey asked.

Cardin Worth cocked her head to the side and considered how much better the day already seemed. "Good morning to you, too."

When she didn't hold out the second cup of coffee for him to take, he came closer. She sipped from her heavy white mug, hiding her grin and her giddy rush of nerves behind it.

But when he stopped in front of her, she made the mistake of lowering her gaze from his face to the exposed strip of his chest. It was either give him his cup of coffee or bury her nose against him and breathe in. She remembered so clearly how he smelled. How he tasted.

She gave him his coffee.

After taking a quick gulp, he smiled and said, "Good morning, Cardin. I hope the floor wasn't too hard for you."

The hardness of the floor hadn't been the problem. She shook her head. "Are you kidding? I slept like a baby, swaddled in my sleeping bag."

"In my sleeping bag, you mean."

If he wanted to get technical, yeah. "Thanks for the loaner. It made sleeping on the floor almost bearable." As had the warmth of his spooned body, she thought, then quickly changed the subject. "I saw you have a loaf of bread and some eggs. Would you like me to cook breakfast?"

He lowered his coffee mug slowly, his gaze as warm as the sun on her shoulders, as the ceramic heating her hands. "I didn't bring you out here to wait on me."

"You didn't bring me out here at all. I volunteered to come."

"To help me get ready for the race. Not to serve me."

"It's just breakfast, Trey. And coffee." Even if last night it had been more. Even if the way he was looking at her made her want to climb back into that sleeping bag. "I work much better when my stomach's not growling. I thought it might be the same for you."

"It is, but I'll cook. You made the coffee."

"That's because I can't work at all without caffeine."

"If I'd known that, I would've put on a pot as soon I got up."

"What time *did* you get up?" Judging by the sun's position, she swore it couldn't be any later than seven now. And, yeah, they'd agreed to start working at six.

"Maybe four?" he guessed, giving her a lazy smile.

"But it was almost two…" She let the sentence dangle, finishing the thought privately. She was quite sure he knew exactly what time they'd finally fallen asleep after he'd made love to her.

The question facing her now was where did this relationship—if you could even call it *that*—go from here?

* * * * *

Cardin and Trey are about to find out that great sex is only the beginning....
Don't miss the fireworks!
Get ready for
A LONG, HARD RIDE
by Alison Kent
Available March 2009,
wherever Blaze books are sold.